BOOK 4 OF THE SANCTUARY CHRONICLES

SANCTUARY

GREG RODE

ISBN: 978-1-957723-52-5

Rode. Greg
Sanctuary

Edited by: Melissa Long
Illustrations by: Merissa Jones

Warren publishing

Published by Warren Publishing
Charlotte, NC
www.warrenpublishing.net
Printed in the United States

To my children, Rebecca and Garrett.
I began all of this for you, to create
something that could last, well, hopefully
forever. Many years later, I'm glad you're
both now old enough to read these,
and more importantly, that you like them.

Don't miss the
The Sanctuary Chronicles
by Greg Rode:

Part I

CHAPTER 1

Spring 2014

I've been bitten ... by a zombie.

This has been my greatest fear since the zombies inherited the earth a couple of years ago and left small groups of survivors like ours scraping out an existence where they can, reliving the ancient past when man had to forage for food and avoid predators. We aren't the top of the food chain anymore; we have turned into one of the lower links, and now we must fight for survival. All day, every day.

After dozens of battles, large and small, and hundreds of zombies killed, I've been bitten on the shoulder by an alpha zombie who had hidden inside the cabin on the remote mountain lake where we've been living in upstate New York. Not all the zombies are alphas, of course, but there are some smart ones mixed in with the people eaters. They somehow direct the others and seem capable of rudimentary strategy. The alpha had ambushed me at the end of the last conflict, when we'd slaughtered his followers, biting me before my sister, Morgan, blew him to smithereens. I've been scraped and scratched a good handful of times across the seemingly never-ending conflicts, but there had never been a real transfer of fluids, which is what we've assumed is how one becomes a zombie. If whatever had caused the zombie beginning and human race ending had been airborne, we'd all be monsters or dead, so fluids make the most sense.

I'm not alone during this time ... at least there's that. Morgan, Eve, and Amy are sitting on the front porch with me, fatigue and anxiety showing on their faces. Our dogs—Ajax and Jack—are draped heavily across the green floorboards like enormous, lumpy rugs. Tongues lolling out of their mouths, they look exhausted from the fight and are covered with the bloody remnants of their conquests. I'm taking it as a good sign that they're not growling at me. Morgan wears the same gory debris from our battle around the lake, where we and the dogs wiped out the last dozen zombies or so before heading back to check on Eve and Amy. Not fighters, they'd hidden in the panic room I'd crafted under the floor of the family room. It was there inside the cabin that the zombie had lurked in the shadows, waiting for us, and launched himself onto my back, tearing a searing chunk of me out with his jagged ravaging teeth until Morgan delivered a shotgun finish that got him off me. We dragged his lifeless—and mostly headless—corpse out of the house, tossed it to the ground like a bag of trash, and then settled on the porch to patch me up and figure out what to do next. Eve holds my pistol awkwardly on her thigh, unused to handling weapons and uneasy with the knowledge that she's the one we've chosen to shoot me in the face if I change. Amy's our preteen companion. She sits in one of the motley collection of chairs scattered across the open space, with her knees tucked up against her chest, arms hugging her legs tightly. Her eyes are darting around under her ever-unkempt blond hair, inspecting our faces as children do when they're unsure of what's happening. We have no assurances to give her.

Our otherwise safe and quiet sanctuary feels tainted. By the smell of cordite and blood hanging in the air, by the scores of dead zombies not far from us, by Ned's stunning betrayal when he'd led all the nearby zombies here to kill us, by the prospect that I'm going to turn into something we've spent the last couple of years killing or avoiding. It hasn't been a good day.

The last few years have been rough. I fled North Carolina not long after the zombies had arrived, heading toward the Catskill area in New York to the family enclave adjacent to a mountain lake and spread over several hundred acres. The property has been in our family since the early 1900s. Eve, DeeDee, and Amelie came with me, though Eve had stopped and stayed behind in Pennsylvania to be with her dying father, and I thought we'd lost her when we drove off to continue the trip. There had been another person in our little group too: Jack. Not the dog Jack—there have been a few Jacks along the way. Human Jack was a piece of shit who'd betrayed us in his own way before being killed by a group of zombies in North Carolina. I might have had something to do with that, but in my defense, he really, really deserved it. It shakes me how even now, when most of humanity is dead or undead, the base instincts of people override the desire to live in peace. The world had been moving down an unsettling path of selfishness, consumption, and greed, but I'd hoped this whole sweeping-the-planet-nearly-clean thing would bring the remaining survivors together in an ironclad bond of us against them. Jack and Ned, and some others along the way, have revealed the lie in that hope.

Finding that the cabin and surrounding area were largely safe upon arrival, DeeDee, Amelie, and I had settled down to wait for Eve, who had promised to join us once her father passed away. Of course, nothing was going to be that simple in the new world. We were stalked by a trio of local survivors with bad intentions about how women should be treated, but we managed to kill them and met another survivor in the process. Top was a career military man who had strolled into our lives with two dogs: Ajax (Rottweiler) and Mabel (Doberman). They stayed with us through a winter worthy of the fables of mountain dwellers of yore—snow pouring down endlessly and confining us to the compact cabin for months of boredom. When spring finally crept out from under the sprawling white blanket of winter, Top, Amelie, and Mabel were slaughtered by a large group of zombies that had done their own gathering in a nearby town. Grief-stricken by their deaths, frightened by the sheer number of the remaining zombies in town, and worried they'd find us soon, DeeDee and I decided to leave, find Eve, and go somewhere new. Unfortunately, I was due for one more heartbreak. As we were leaving, DeeDee stumbled upon and was stung by hundreds of yellowjackets boiling out of a ground nest in the driveway. That would have been miserable enough for her, but she was allergic to their sting. There was nothing I could do. She died in my arms and left me broken and alone with Ajax and the goddamn voice in my head singing Three Dog Night songs, wondering what to do next.

Ooh, ooh, I know that one! I've got this! One ….

Inertia had smothered me at first, but I wasn't alone for long. First there was Morgan's arrival with the dog Jack (German shepherd) via Corvette from across the country. Then within the same day, Eve, Amy, and Ned trudged in on foot. Eve's father had died not long after we'd left her in Pennsylvania, but the same howling winter that had scoured New York covered the entire Northeast and kept her confined there until it was safe to travel. Ned and Amy had literally stumbled upon her in the early stages of winter, and they all stayed together until the weather permitted them to make the trip to join me. Things had been fine at first despite a rough beginning between Morgan and Eve—though, most people have a rough beginning, middle, and end with Morgan, so that wasn't a shock—but Ned was infatuated with Eve. Eve and I had a largely unspoken connection with an indeterminate destination, and Ned didn't like that, so he led the nearby zombie group to come kill us. Not so fast, however; Ned was killed by those selfsame zombies. Eve and Amy hid in a sheltering room under the floor boards while Morgan and I whittled down the large group in a mad chase around the lake and then wiped the remnants out in the blueberry fields across the water.

And now, here we are. Every story has an ending, I just didn't think mine was going to end with me being bitten by a zombie.

***

We mope around for an hour. I tune into my body, seeking some hidden ache or twinge that's going to be a precursor to me losing my mind to the endless rage and hunger that consumes all the zombies. The dogs keep still for awhile—which includes not biting me to smithereens, so still a good sign—but then rouse themselves, shake, and trot off the porch to do whatever it is dogs abruptly decide to do.

The women stay with me. Morgan is cleaning one of our (many) other pistols on a table but glances over at me intermittently. Amy dozes off in her chair, her breath a soothing susurrus as she settles and sleeps off the terror of having recently been trapped in a safe place. Eve keeps watch, brown eyes fixed firmly on my face, though I sense she's not watching for a change in me but just looking in that curious way she has of studying people rather frankly and with the directness children have. I wonder what she's thinking but don't ask since our relationship has never quite figured itself out, and if I'm going to turn into a people eater who immediately gets its head shot off, I don't want the last thing she tells me to be that she really does like me. Or doesn't. Guess either one would suck at this point, so silence is golden, thank you very much.

Amy budges first, waking with a start and a gasp when a hummingbird buzzes her. I'd fallen prey to that prank myself many times over the years. My grandmother had been fond of little critters—less so little human critters. Hummingbirds and chipmunks were her favorites, so she always had a feeder hanging from the porch and a bag of unshelled peanuts at the ready. The lounge chair in the corner closest to the swimming area was the ugliest sunflower-patterned, hard-cushioned, bare-armrested thing you'd ever sat on, but it also had a hidden tractor beam of sleep that sucked you down without fail. The feeder for the hummingbirds, however, was immediately above the headrest, and when the little monsters came divebombing in for a snack, it would scare the shit out of an innocent sleeper thinking they were being attacked by wasps. Not that I ever thought this was an intentional placement of said feeder. We've kept up the tradition by filling it with sugar water since we arrived.

"This is boring," Amy says, stifling a heavy yawn with the back of her arm. "Those dead things stink really nasty. And I'm hungry."

"God yes, I'm hungry, too," chimes in Morgan, standing up. "C'mon, let's go put some food together. Eve, need anything?"

"No, I'm okay, thanks for asking."

A pause, and then I pipe up. "Hey, thanks, I'm not hungry either." Let's not count me dead or a monster just yet, people.

Morgan looks at me—really, they all do—a bit nonplussed. "Good point," she says. "We need to find something to do with you while we're waiting for something or nothing to happen. We can't babysit you overnight, not safely, and who knows how long this is going to take. We have to clean up this … this mess," she says with a wave toward the scattered corpses defiling our peaceful home.

She wanders off toward the detached garage that also holds our grandfather's tools and returns a few minutes later with a roll of duct tape. "This should work," she says with something of a smirk and tells Amy to climb off the lounger. "We'll wrap you up so that if something happens, the worst thing you can do is hop around with thirty pounds of chair attached to your back like a zombie pogo stick. Or roll around on the floor moaning. That might actually be funny."

Ah, my sister, gotta love her.

Most of the time.

It's a good idea though. It'll free them all up to clean the place without having to keep an eye on me. I don't like the thought that nudges about how if I *do* change while I'm alone with the dogs, it may be a very unpleasant ending since I'll be unable to run or fight. So I hope that if I change, all my marbles go sayonara along the way rather than be aware as I'm getting killed by the canines of canines.

Morgan's at least nice enough to run the first wraps of the tape around me with the sticky side out, and then winds a second series of bands sticky-side down, right over that, binding me tight to the frame of the lounger without the prospect of removing a ton of my skin if I end up okay and need to be set free. I'm completely unable to move, with three silver stripes around my legs and two trapping my arms to my torso and chair.

As she works, Morgan takes a trip down memory lane. "Hey, this reminds me of that time me and the girls tied you—"

I immediately recall what she's beginning to talk about and interrupt her sharply. "Not now, Morgan."

"No, wait, this is a funny story, remember? This'll cheer everyone up. Me and Trina and Cassie were high school seniors, and you were a freshman. We made you sit in a chair and tied you up because we were going to put makeup on you and do your hair. You went along with it at first, but then you got a bone—"

"*Really* not the time, Morgan!" I'm not sure whether to shout or plead and desperately look over at Eve to see how closely she's paying attention. Sadly, she is and has the hint of a smile tucked into the corner of her pretty face. While it's nice to see her smile, the rest of this particular story only gets worse for me. "C'mon, I just got bit by a fucking zombie, might die, might turn into one of them, and you're dragging *this* story out of the memory banks? You can tell them after I die, okay?"

I can't help but travel down that memory's path though. Like memories sometimes do, it suddenly launches to mind with complete clarity and plays like a video clip in my head. Morgan had some hot friends when we were younger; they all played sports but were the pretty clique within the team who also made the effort to doll up when the time was right. None of those friends was hotter than Cassie, who had cascades of curly red hair and a killer curvy and athletic figure she was more than aware of and liked to show off. I had a hopeless crush on her for years and went out of my way to insert myself—not that way, though I wished—into whatever the girls were doing when possible, just to be near her, smell her, watch her. Even dorky stuff like allowing them to play dress-up with me. In high school.

Not exactly a little-known fact: the teenage penis takes zero prompting, and as the girls had been tying me up and then running their hands through my then-long hair, I got an erection that stood at miserable, and visible, attention. It had been impossible to miss, and while the girls had squealed and stepped away at first, after a couple of minutes, they continued to torture me, and I continued to sit there, bound and more miserable—in more ways than one—than I had ever been. Did I partly hope they would shoo my sister from the room and take wild sexual advantage of me? Of course. Was I also terrified they would do exactly that? You bet your ass.

Luckily, this predated the full proliferation of smartphones with handy cameras and social media because it would've been too easy for pictures to get into the viral-about-everything high school network. The girls also never told their other friends as far as I know. So I'd emerged unscathed but went through the rest of that school year with the touch of fear all kids have about "that moment" going public and ruining their lives. After the girls had graduated, they all went to remote colleges. I never saw Cassie again, and this story had fallen into the past.

Until now. Thanks, sis.

Hey, I remember that time too! She was sooo nice to look at, and I'm pretty sure she had a little thing for you, too, but you were too young. That body, whew, just curves all over the place. And all those tight clothes she wore all the time? Damn. Hey now, is that a little something coming to life down below the belt? Is it? Oh, how funny that would be in front of three more women. Can you manage cold thoughts? Can you not think about her? Can you keep the little chubster down? This is some funny shit! Let her tell the rest. I really, really want to see how this turns out!

"Okay, fine, but only because Amy's here," Morgan says, clearly a bit disappointed to not complete my humiliation in front of a new audience. "But I might have to tell Eve the rest later on. It was some afternoon."

Right about then, I decide that if I change, and if I manage to get off the goddamn lounger and free, the first person I'm going to bite is Morgan. And if I don't change, I'm going to find out how long she can hold her breath underwater in the lake. For crying out loud, maybe it'll be better if someone does have to shoot me in the face since that isn't the full story, and it absolutely gets worse.

She finishes and steps back, surveying her work and nodding her head. "You're not going anywhere. We've got work to do, so, you know, sit tight!"

Smartass.

***

They leave me, go inside to eat, and then come out to busy themselves with the task of cleaning up. I wouldn't have eaten first myself since it's a mess in every direction.

I face the driveway and parking area from my confined seat and see at least a half-dozen bodies strewn about and know there are a handful more behind me. When Ned had led the army of the dead—*I see what you did there*—to us, Morgan and I had fired a few rounds here while Eve and Amy fled to the panic room built beneath the floorboards of the main cabin. We then led the rest of them in a chase around the path circling the lake, pausing intermittently to whittle them down. That had been a great strategy, but it also left a breadcrumb trail of dead zombies for almost a mile. My grandfather's BMW sits at the top of the driveway at an angle, with the notch and fletching of the embedded crossbow bolt barely visible in the driver's door. I guess that whatever's left of Ned is just behind the door. As Ned had prematurely celebrated his "victory" over us, Morgan shot him through the door, pinning him there, and he found out the hard way how much zombies like the smell of blood and an easy meal. Poor planning, Ned, you asshole.

Eve and Morgan do most of the work since the bodies are heavy. Most of them are adults, but Amy drags a boy who's about her size past me, holding him by the ankles. He's facedown and leaves a trail of murky gore behind as she hauls him across the scant grass of our lawn. There's zombie goo everywhere, and I hope it will rain soon, and hard, to clean it all up. The women bring the wheelbarrow out of the garage, load one body at a time, and wheel it over to the truck we have. Then one of them clambers up into the bed to drag the corpse into a growing pile of grisly limbs and torsos. A drizzle of their commingled viscous blood runs slowly down the gutters stamped in the steel surface, pattering out of a corner and onto the dusty surface of the driveway to soak slowly in. We'll be digging that out as well when all the work is done. While we've probably gotten all of them, they're definitely drawn by the scent of blood, like shambling sharks with legs, so all of it has to go.

For a while, I watch them but eventually get bored myself since I'm unable to help. I'm horrible at sitting still to begin with; I always need to be doing something, so being forced to do nothing is even worse. I slide into some kind of a fugue where I'm watching them but not really paying attention to anything other than their movements, in a tangential way. Normally, I find that falling into old, familiar memories is a comforting distraction technique when I'm under stress, but now my thoughts are a jumble between memory, regret, a touch of fear, and wondering what if.

I'm too young to die. Like, fifty years too young. I want to be able to protect and lead my little tribe, to keep them safe and happy and able to rely on me. Dead me or zombie me—which seems the more likely of the two since I feel fine aside from the nagging discomfort in my shoulder where I've been munched—isn't going to be able to do any of those things. So, I'm alone with my thoughts, which isn't always a good thing. Like anyone with a busy mind, there are times when my thoughts can wander off into ridiculous directions.

Like anyone who goes through high school, college, and complicated relationships during those years, I feel bad for any feelings I've hurt along the way. Various faces and names drift to mind, like shimmering reflections on water, from Lisa to Jackie to Summer, girls I'd been fairly serious with and then moved on from in the way young people do. I'm less selfish now and regret not having the perspective I've gained in the ensuing years. The truth may sting more sharply than some half-assed it's-me-not-you kind of explanation, but then the pain goes away more quickly since there's no wondering. It's something that may have done some good in the current world—well, current before the zombies, of course—where everyone tiptoes around, trying not to offend anyone, and ends up not saying anything specific enough to get anywhere. Say what you mean and mean what you say. It saves a lot of bullshit.

I'm sad for the loss of music. Sure, we can play it on battery-powered gadgets since batteries are now wicked cheap (free) and should be good for another few years at least, and there's a massive clearance sale at every music store (again, free). But that means background noise, and background noise hides zombie-invasion noise, so it's a bad idea. Music was a constant companion for me in the old days, especially since I was often alone as I crept into my later twenties. It was always on in the house, always on in the car; I took it with me everywhere, and it took me everywhere too. There was little I enjoyed more than listening to a song and recollecting the memory tied to it. That time when I spent the night driving around with a carload of friends, the windows open in the New York summer, tunes blaring, laughter cascading out into the dark, and feeling carefree and never-ending in the world of music and memory. That time when I kissed a girl for the first time, my heart racing, feeling nervous as hell, excited as hell, and terrified I was going to be a bad kisser and drool down the sides of our interlocked mouths—yep, but I know I'm not the only one to have to figure that out. Those times.

Whether it's a fast-paced metal gallop, classic rock anthem, or soaring power ballad, I feel incomplete without music. My favorite had been when I was running. Not a major skill for me; I liked to run for a fairly long time but not fast, just a stubborn jog for as long as I could stand it, and creating intricate playlists for an hour-long outing made me a happy pavement pounder and took my mind off the tedium. About the only place I left it behind was the golf course. Golf was difficult enough for me without any additional distraction.

I'm disappointed no one's going to make a new *Star Wars* movie to undo the wrongs wrought on the franchise in the "second" trilogy. Here, the memories are a comfort; I can still recall clearly watching the very first one on vacation in Myrtle Beach and being just blown away, speechless at first and then amazed and then babbling about it for weeks to my parents, asking them questions they couldn't have known the answer to.

Now, hold on a minute. You're maybe dying or going to turn into a flesh-gobbling lunatic, and you're wasting our time thinking about freaking Star Wars *movies? What is* wrong *with you?*

Just let me wander around memory lane in peace, will you?

I wish I'd tried the things that were once on my to-do list, which now remain on my to-didn't list. Writing a novel is one; some way to give that same feeling I get from a good book to others. That feeling where you get closer to the end, even though you know it's coming by the dwindling number of pages, and try to ignore the fact that the curtain is coming down. I always got a kick out of movies that were kind enough to give something of a teaser segue into what happened afterward, and I wished books had done that from time to time. You know, something like: "Bobby went back to school, finished his degree, married Lori, and lived happily ever after." Those closing credits.

I've always thought that the ideal would be if I wrote a book, and it found its way into the hands of one of the authors I loved, and *they* actually enjoyed it. That would've been pretty damn skippy.

If I could have given back a little bit of what I'd gotten from reading over the years, I'd have been a happy camper. I tried in the past to write an action-adventure-spy kind of thing. I actually even had some of it typed out and everything. There was just that teeny, tiny problem with the fucking lights being out everywhere and my book hiding in the now-dormant cyberworld without a way to get it out. Besides, what would I do now? Write a book by hand? Drunken doctors writing with their opposite hand have better handwriting than I do, and like everyone else, I can type far faster than I can write, thanks to the office job.

I wish I'd done more traveling. I was something of a content homebody who liked routine and sanity since work had always been anything but routine and sane over the years. Now, however, travel has become dangerous for different reasons than it had been in the past, though I suppose the entire country, or continent, is up for grabs if we're so motivated. Maybe we could get a beach house? My grandparents had been snowbirds my entire life, traveling on the long weekends that bracketed the summer, between here and Cocoa Beach in Florida. Warm zombies are active and, therefore, unpleasant zombies, but there are enough coastal islands in the Carolinas that could maybe be barricaded across the access bridges to keep them out. We could sweep them clean, live there for the cooler months, and then retreat here in the summer months. Something to think about.

Like Eve in a bathing suit again. That's another something to think about. Well, technically, a couple of somethings, if you know what I mean. Road trip!

Sigh.

***

The day carries on while I wander around aimlessly inside my head, going everywhere across my life and considering choices I made that pushed me this way and that; some of them were good decisions and some more like those Morgan had selected. All of them had arguably worked out well enough, I suppose, but I kill time taking the paths not taken to keep my mind off things.

Funny, that. I think about things to keep my mind off things.

It begins to cool down, and sharply, in the way evening falls here. The sun drifts lazily to just above the western tree line, and their shadows spike across the flat silver surface of the lake to paint a double image that's worthy of a postcard. If there are postcards left. Or people to mail them to. Or mailmen. Jesus. Well, he's probably not here either.

All the cleanup is finally finished. At least, as far as loading the nearby bodies into the bed of the truck with Ned's body—what's left of it—mixed in there somewhere. The women make their way back to the porch to rest and check on me. The dogs trot up, nudge my captive hands with their muzzles—quizzical looks on their faces—and then go indoors to settle on their beds near the fireplace. It has been a very long day for all of us.

"How are you holding up? You've been pretty quiet up here, which, I guess, is a good thing." It was Eve, with worry and fatigue stitched across her face.

"Well enough, I guess, though hungry and thirsty and, truth be told, kind of need the outhouse," I answer.

She looks startled a bit at that, as does Morgan over her shoulder, who speaks next. "Oops. We didn't think about that, but no way are we cutting you loose. Maybe you're a sneaky, next-level zombie who can talk. Sorry, little brother, but you're just going to have to go right where you are. Food and water, we can do, though you try and nibble one of us, and it's go time."

"Morgan, I've been meaning to tell you this for a long time. You are my least favorite sister, you know that?" I'm half-serious since she's my only sister of course, but her casual tone bothers me. There's a chance I'm going to die, or turn and die, and the one person here who has been with me for my entire life is making jokes. I know she's making jokes out of nerves, and likely to try and keep me relaxed, but still.

She looks at me carefully, reading my tone and getting the message. Her face softens, and I can see the strain she's feeling and her concern for me. "I'm sorry," she says slowly, clearly organizing her thoughts about what she's going to say. "I'm freaked out. I don't want to lose you, I don't think I can handle it. You've been the one … the *only* one who has accepted and loved me as me. Mom and Dad, they tried, and I know they loved me as much as they could, but I think part of that was because that's how it works. You have to love your kids. It's a rule. Even the wild ones like me who had to live every minute like it was the only one, and it was *my* minute and no one else's. I know, I get it. But you, even though it's the same rule for siblings, you love me because that's how you're made up. Once you do love someone, it's unbreakable no matter what, and you'd die before surrendering one of 'your' people."

She pauses for a breath, pulling it in shakily. "I've been able to count on you, even when I didn't reach out to you. I knew you would be there, and you'd tell me it was okay, that I was going to be all right no matter what crazy shit I'd gotten myself into, and that was almost as good as hearing your actual voice telling me all of that. I'd picture the conversation in my mind and always knew you'd tell me it was no big deal, or you weren't upset with me, something along those lines. You really are who we all lean on. It doesn't happen a lot to me, but I'm scared. Scared to lose you and to see what would happen to us without you here."

Whoa. I think I already knew all that inside my head, but for her to spill it all out means she's really frightened, which does not come naturally to Morgan. "Morgan," I say, looking directly at her and then at Eve and Amy in turn. "It *is* going to be okay. Even if something happens to me, you three are going to be okay here. It's safe now. We got them all. You could be here for as long as you want."

No one says anything for a long minute. We all just look around at each other in silence. I realize I'm more worried about them than I am about me. She's right.

"You're still not getting off the chair for a potty break."

Aaaand, she's back. So much for having a moment.

***

After they go inside, eat their dinner, and clean up, they start getting settled for bedtime. I'm able to watch them bustle about indoors since I'm facing back toward the driveway, parallel to the house and lakefront. We've found ourselves more attuned to the sun rising and setting than people had been in the recent past, when we'd simply get up when the sun emerged and wind down quickly after sunset. No more daylight savings time to foul up our internal clocks for a week, no movies to stay up late and watch, just a more natural rhythm with the world.

Morgan eventually drifts back out onto the porch, carrying a dark gray wool blanket that I've slept under since I was two feet tall, and wordlessly wraps it around me, tucking it in to confine me even further. Since we usually visited on the Labor or Memorial Day weekends bookending the summer when we were kids, it had always been colder here than it had been farther south in New York at night. We'd rarely be down to shorts and a T-shirt after dinnertime and would huddle under the freezing sheets, shivering and our teeth chattering for a few minutes, trying not to move until our body heat warmed us up enough. It's going to be cold overnight, and I suppose I'm going to have my first campout. By myself. Even the dogs choose to go indoors, which is normal but tells me where I am in the who-is-the-favorite-human pecking order.

And so I sit still, waiting for some indication from my body that I'm in trouble, while the late evening surrenders its shadows and falls to the blackened carpet of night. It isn't quiet, nor is it fully dark since the stars flicker brightly in the sky, which has always been clearer here than in the cities. The lack of human combustion and business for well over a year had made all skies a sharper, cleaner blue. Various nighttime sounds—chipmunks, birds, and whatever else wanders around after we've gone to sleep—rustle in the rhododendron patches behind me, at first making me skittish until I remember we've killed all the dangerous creatures, and so I ignore them.

Alone in the dark; alone in my thoughts. More meandering around in the mental history books, though more so on the recent past of DeeDee, Top, and Amelie. I should have done things differently with Amelie; we should have kept her in the main cabin with us after she and Top had been ambushed, but I never contemplated that someone her age would dash off alone for revenge and be slaughtered along with Mabel. There's some guilt lingering about DeeDee, too, though I couldn't have done anything about her allergy to the hundreds of yellowjacket stings she'd gotten as we were trying to leave. But if I hadn't been so exhausted from running to and from the town to try to chase down Amelie, maybe I would have been on that side of the truck and taken the stings myself, and she'd still be alive. Maybe, shoulda, coulda, woulda. Lots of those have piled up over the years.

And then, of course, my mind takes me down the path of what the future will look like if I don't die (really doubting that) or turn—possible, which will be followed by dying, so … well shit. Will we stay here? It's safe now, it's familiar ground that will always give us an advantage for defense if there are other invasions, the cold will keep our winters unadventurous except for dealing with the elements and cabin fever, and we have fresh water and farms nearby we can resurrect and enjoy. It's sanctuary, not like the false one Morgan drove through back in Kansas, but a real one. Will we find more people? Will Eve and I ever move beyond this weird spot we're in and become a couple? What will things be like in five years? Ten? I picture us all getting older here like my grandparents had, taking walks around the lake after lunch, though eschewing walking sticks for shotguns and pistols. Children? What about that? I like to think I'd make a good parent, but I suppose some of the early life lessons will be a bit different than what I learned in the past.

That stuff, however, I will definitely be good at. I imagine sitting with a toddler on my lap and, after reading a book or working on a puzzle, going over how to clean a pistol, shoot a zombie, escape a horde, and so on. At least the children will gather a host of actual hands-on abilities beyond what I've seen of kids in my old neighborhood, who had largely seemed skilled with their thumbs on their gadgets. I guess, to be fair, I have a different perspective since the evolution of the phone and other handhelds had come after my youth, and I can understand how access to anything would be tempting. I like to think I'd put them down to do something physical, but I suppose you never know, and I'm not going to find out since they're all useless paperweights now.

I lose track of time and begin to doze off, which surprises me when I pop back up.

Here I am, waiting to maybe call it my last day as a human, and I'm drifting off to sleep. Yeah, it has been a big day, and I'm physically beat and emotionally wrought, so it makes sense. I play the game of my head drifting back toward the cushion, snapping up, repeat for what feels like an hour until I'm finally fully asleep. My last thought before falling away from the world is that for the first time in my life, I'm afraid of the future since there's a good chance I'm closer to the end than the beginning.

***

What wakes me is the weight. Hard to gauge through the wool blanket and my pants, but it begins at my left ankle and slowly, steadily winds its way up the crease made by my legs. This is it then. This is how it happens. Starting at your feet and creeping up along your body until it takes over your brain, and you're a zombie. My heart rate throttles up to about five hundred beats per minute, and I wonder if you're trapped inside the shell of what used to be you, conscious and aware but unable to stop the monster raging across the world, searching for food and more food. I begin to panic and almost start to thrash against the tape binding me, but then abruptly remember I'd been bitten in the shoulder, not lower, and if I'm going to catch anything, it makes sense that the infection would begin up there. I freeze because I figure out what's happening, and if there's anything I'm more afraid of than a zombie bite, it's this.

A snake.

I hate snakes. No, I should clarify that. I hate surprise snakes; ones "over there" aren't horrible, but I still don't like them. My mother was terrified of snakes when we were growing up, and being out in the country in New York meant there had been one or two every summer to contend with, though rarely a poisonous one. There was one episode that scared me terribly when I was about ten. I'd been in the lake, floating off the dock in an inner tube—and, therefore, about as nimble as a turtle on its back—when a black snake rose out of the water and swam toward me, mouth open like a goddamn sea monster. I panicked, flailing wildly around but uncertain whether to paddle away, flip myself over— which would've put me in the water, no, thank you—or just wait to die. My uncle had been standing on the dock and reached down, plucked me out of the tube by the arm, and saved the day. After that, every snake was target practice with the BB guns we were allowed to have. I rarely have dreams in much detail to where I can remember them in the mornings, but the recurring one I carried with me after that incident was of being out in the middle of the lake in a powerboat, looking over the side, and seeing the surface of the lake completely covered in a writhing, coiling sheet of horror. Luckily, the dream had been confined to the lake I'd grown up on, not this one.

North Carolina, being a warmer climate, has more snakes and a higher count of dangerous ones, like copperheads and rattlesnakes, though I was fortunate to never come across one of those. Most common are what turned out to be earth snakes, little ones maybe six to ten inches long, no fatter than a finger, and a light brownish gray. Their scientific name is *holy shit, it's a fucking snake right there ... oh, never mind, it's another earth snake.* I would run into those fairly often when doing yard work, and when I could, I swept them into a bucket and then into the yard-waste bin so they'd be carried off to wherever it was the grass clippings, leaves, and sticks went. I never killed them, despite my fear and loathing, which is something I've never understood about myself. I really, *really* don't like snakes, and logically, that means any of them I see should be snake confetti, but the part of me that runs the show deeper inside has decided that killing things unnecessarily isn't okay. Yeah, makes no sense.

But now, I have one winding its way up my body in the dark, and it's not a tiny snake. I can't see it at all because nights now are absolute pitch-black—much darker than in the past—so I just feel its sinuous progress up toward my lap. I rack my skittering brain, trying to remember if there are any poisonous ones up here, and can't recall ever coming across a serious one; only very rarely over the years would we see a black snake, and even those had been small ones no more than a foot or two long. Whatever's on my lap is much bigger than that since I can feel pressure from ankles to waist, and its weight is solid, pressing the blankets down.

I fight the urge to completely lose my shit. Not that I can move much given the tape bindings, but I try to keep my breathing slow and steady, which is no small trick given the fear clambering into my head like a gargoyle scaling a building. Images of being bitten, a reticulating maw gaping and lunging with fangs bared and dripping with death, claw their insistent way into my thoughts. I'm going to have a heart attack before it can finish me off, and I'm going to be okay with that; anything would be better than death by snakebite. At least if it bites me now, I won't see it coming, which somehow makes it better. I'm horrified by the vision of a strike coming toward my face. Though now that I've gone there, the vision of it happening in the dark is no better.

It stops, right in my lap, and I feel it begin circling into a coil, and finally, all motion ceases. Being bitten in the dick is no more appetizing, but at least I have the blanket and my pants to guard that area. I suddenly realize it's seeking warmth, not food. I have an invisible, unknown snake in my lap, and it's going to take a freaking nap? The fear retreats a bit, though now I'm afraid I'm going to sneeze, fart, or something, and it's going to get me. I've never been more focused on being immobile in my life, sitting there wrapped in a duct-tape prison, with a zombie bite on my shoulder and a who-knows-what-kind-it-is snake snoozing in my lap. I think I'd rather turn into a zombie than anything else.

Today has so not been my day.

***

The sun rises from behind the cabin and the steep hillside that shades it, so morning creeps along gradually here. I didn't realize I'd fallen asleep, but I awake with a start as the birds begin to welcome another day. I then immediately close my eyes as I recall I have a pet in my lap who is certain to bite me now that I've moved.

Nothing.

I keep my eyes closed; better to be attacked without seeing.

Still nothing.

I feel nothing in my lap, though I notice at the same time that my legs are asleep, and so I finally peek cautiously out of the corner of one eye, ready to close it again. It's gone. Nothing left behind but a circular recess in the blanket and some dusty scales where it had rested before apparently deciding to move along. I take a leak, right there in my pants on my grandmother's lounge chair, in celebration.

The details of the morning become more visible, from silhouettes to monochrome outlines and shapes to tentative colors coming to life. I sit—not like I have any alternatives— and watch the lake, our home, the vehicles in the driveway, and all the pieces of the place I've found the most comforting in my life. I am shamelessly happy to be alive, with perhaps a tear or two sneaking down my cheeks, and thankful we have our sanctuary and that, despite all the loss in the recent past, I now have my sister, Eve, Amy, and the dogs. Throw in a white picket fence and a couple of kids, and it'd be the American dream, right? I'm also thankful it has been more than twelve hours since I've been bitten, and I'm still me. Aside from some achiness in my shoulder from the trauma of the zombie bite, everything feels great. Looks like I'm going to make it.

Bumps from inside the cabin inform that the others are waking up too. A few moments later, Ajax and Jack burst with a clatter out the front door, sniff me briefly, and then go off to water the grass. They bark happily at nothing whatsoever and trot out of my sight to inspect the day. Next one outside is Morgan, rubbing sleep from her eyes and with a spectacular case of bed head forming a tri-pointed mohawk angled toward the sky. She takes a good long look at me and then smiles. "Not a zombie!"

"No, not a zombie," I reply. "Cold, hungry, and not very well rested, but not a zombie."

"That's good. I really didn't want to have to shoot you. I might've wanted to a few times back when we were teenagers, but not so much now."

"Gee, Morgan, you have a heart of gold, don't you? Cut me loose."

"Oh, I don't know, I kind of like you as a captive audience. When Eve wakes up, I can tell her the rest of the story about Cassie. She'll want to hear that. C'mon, it'll be fun!"

I'm going to kill her. Well, I'm going to kill her if she's dumb enough to let me out of my tape. "Morgan, for the love of God, cut this fucking tape off of me so I can get up and kill you."

With that, she unleashes the full power of her smile and retrieves a knife from one of the painted side tables dotting the porch, and comes over to slice me free. "I'm glad you're okay. We all are," she says as she pulls the blanket off and flicks the razor-sharp knife through the silver tape straps along my body until I'm loose.

I stand and hug her as tightly as I can without crushing her (though it's tempting), smelling her hair and feeling the warmth of the bed, then step back and smile myself. I'm okay, not a zombie and not bitten by a snake. It's all good. Like most bad times in life, the sun rises the next day, you wake up, the coffee is still delicious, your car starts, and you go to work or wherever. It's not a lot different than the day before except for whatever pieces of the prior day you now carry with you.

"Hey," my tender, caring, sweet sister says, "you smell like piss." Wisely, she immediately scampers off the porch to safety before the circulation fully resumes in my legs.

CHAPTER 2

There's still a lot of work to do. The BMW is blocking the top of the driveway, so we can't haul the corpses piled into the back of the pickup out until I move the car off to the side parking area through the gore that was splattered in all directions during Ned's death. I can't find the keys in the ignition or on the ground nearby, so I make a mental note to dig through his pockets when we dump the bodies. My guess is that, like any creature of habit, after he'd turned the car off, he subconsciously slipped the keys into a pants pocket. He isn't near the top of the stack in the truck, and there's no way I'm going to bother excavating him now. Too grisly and too much chance something is alive in there, even a bit, and I've hit my quota for zombie bites.

My grandfather would have been ripping pissed about his car. The crossbow bolt tore a quarter-sized hole in the door on entry, punching through the inner panel and perforating Ned's leg to pin him in place. But all his thrashing about widened the damage to both holes, not to mention left sprays of blood on the seat, carpet, and window glass. That's going to take some time to clean up, but I'm going to do it. The car had been special to me as a kid, and since Ned did one good thing and got it running, I want to be able to cruise around in it; not to mention that having another vehicle in addition to the truck and Corvette is beneficial. I slip it into neutral and push it out of the way so we can get the truck and its grim cargo out.

Eve is awake by now, though Amy's not. Teenagers can sleep through anything. Morgan has decided to stay back with the dogs and keep watch in case we didn't kill all the monsters after all, so Eve and I clamber into the truck to bring the bodies down to where we'd disposed of the bodies of the three men who had tried to take DeeDee and Amelie what feels like so long ago. Those three died in the driveway too. As I'm reminiscing about that brawl, I regret we'd been in such a spot that forced Amelie to be a killer as a teen. Unfortunately, I acknowledge we'll have to do the same with Amy and, to some extent, Eve. No way can Morgan and I continue to do all the fighting, not while being worried about those two being safe. It'll distract us if we're ever out in the open, and we'll fight differently and risk us all being killed.

Peeking over at Eve while I'm driving the fully loaded Ford as delicately as I can up the ruts of the driveway so I won't spill any of the messy detritus, I decide to hold off on that conversation for now. She still looks sleepy herself, with a peaceful expression on her face, though she also doesn't look fully in the moment either as she gazes out the windshield into the fern-dotted undergrowth aside the road. "Penny for your thoughts?"

"Where did that expression come from, I wonder," she says. "I mean, depending on the thought, it might be worth a lot more than a penny."

"No clue but good point. When online search engines come back to life, we can find out since the internet holds all the truths. Are you okay?"

I see her turn toward me as I drive out onto the "main" road, which is really just a fancier dirt road than the driveway. She doesn't say anything for a couple of moments, just seems to be looking at me, so I wait. That's one thing I have in ample supply: patience. After all, we aren't in a rush for anything anymore. There's no job to get to, all the gadgets that had chirped or buzzed or flickered for our attention are permanently asleep, most watches have run down their batteries, and survival doesn't have a schedule. We follow the rhythms of the day, and that's about it.

"I'm okay," she finally says. "I was just thinking how delicate this all is. There are just the four of us, and we just got lucky, I think, both in the fight and with you not being killed or turned. That we'd be safer if we had more people, to where if we lost one, we wouldn't be crippled." She stops speaking, and I see her shift sideways in her seat to face me, removing her seat belt as she does so. Funny how we mostly still wear seat belts out of both habit and need—when you run over a zombie, you tend to get bounced around a bit. "We can't afford to lose anyone, and I really can't bear the thought of losing you. I didn't sleep at all last night. I just lay there in bed, waiting for you to start raving in the chair, or for the morning to come and I'd find you dead. I kept wanting to come check on you, but I was afraid."

She drops off to silence again.

Normally, I'd have kept driving and talking, but this feels like a moment, so I stop the truck, put it into park, and shed my own seat belt. Way back in North Carolina, she'd broached a delicate topic, and I wasn't direct with my answer. That bothered me then and from time to time since, so I'm going to be fully engaged now. Way back in the beginning, when we were semitrapped by the queen alpha zombie, who wanted us to have children for her to eat in exchange for our safety, we couldn't figure out a good way to kill her and her followers. The two of us went on a drive in search of dynamite, and at one point, Eve subtly offered to get pregnant to buy us time. I'm cautious, and perhaps skittish, enough with normal relationships, let alone ones in this new world, and was so stunned that I weakly dodged the topic. "Eve, we're going to be okay, and I'm not going anywhere. I'm going to be here until the end, whenever that is, and I'm going to watch over you and the others to my last breath. You can bet your bottom dollar on that."

"Another expression that doesn't make a ton of sense," she says with a grin. "But I'm going to hold you to that."

She leans across the cab of the truck, and I fold her compact form into my arms, snugging her tight to me. I'm used to having her close from way back in the beginning, when she came in my room to sleep beside me every so often, but that had been for company. She hugs me back, and as we break, she kisses me carefully on the lips. Not a fooling around kiss, not that simple, but something else that's more complicated. It doesn't last for long, but I have a feeling as we separate that I'm going to remember it for the rest of my days, however many of those I'm lucky enough to get. I hold her gaze for what feels like minutes; there isn't anything to say or do, she isn't looking for a different kind of kiss, and I'm not either. This isn't the time, if there's ever going to be a time. We rely on each other, we've been together the longest, and there's a thing there, but it isn't going to change right now.

I slide the truck back into gear and resume the trek down the hill, steering with my left hand as I've always done. Eve reaches across the bench seat and wordlessly takes my other hand in hers. And so we drive on, holding hands like kids, hauling a cargo of corpses, abominations and a traitor, to dump. What an absolutely batshit world we're living in, but at least we're living.

***

It's just the start of another long day. After dumping the first load down in the valley near the now-decomposing and picked-over-by-animals bodies of the other three men—hard to not look out of the corner of your eye, even though you know it's going to be nasty—we drive back home and gather Morgan, Amy, and the dogs to go around the lake and get the rest of them. I've fished the keys to the BMW out of Ned's pocket, trying very hard not to look closely at what little is left of him either after the zombies had worked him over rather spectacularly.

Clearing out the shooting range where Morgan and I had made our stand requires the least effort since it's reachable by one of the dirt roads, and we can get there in the truck, but the bodies littered on the smaller path that circles the lake are a pain in the ass. We park at one of the other cabins, find a wheelbarrow, navigate over the rocks and roots that are everywhere, and then collect the dead.

By the time we're done with the final load and head back home, it's twilight and cooling off again. At least I'm not going to sleep outside again tonight, but we're, in a way, back to the beginning. Safe, quiet, but now what?

CHAPTER 3

The four of us spend the next few days cleaning up the mess inside the cabin left by the splattered zombie head, the driveway for the blood and gore spilled at the beginning of the fight, and the bed of the truck after disposal. When we finally finish, aside from the big hole in the door of the car and the absence of Ned, it's as if nothing had happened. We want to scout farther afield to make sure all the monsters have come to the ball, and since the BMW and Corvette are too small, we arm ourselves heavily, and then all six of us pile into the truck and go to town. The dogs, like all dogs, love to ride in the back, ears and tongues flapping in the breeze, and taking it all in with happy barks for no reason whatsoever. I guess, sometimes, barking is just fun.

The town is quiet, perfectly quiet. I drive with Morgan riding shotgun and windows down so we can hear anything. I coast through the main streets in neutral as often as I can at first, just listening. We cross back and forth for over an hour, even though it's a small place to begin with, hitting all the side streets and honking the horn from time to time to see if we can bring out the dead or, less likely, the living. Nothing, even where we saw them gathering before in some sort of central point.

One thing that has been nagging at me for a while is how they survived the winter months without a food supply. It had been a miserable winter by any standards, with feet of snow dumped on the entire region. We were fine enough in the cabin, cold but fine, and with adequate food and firewood to make it bearable. Going to the bathroom wasn't as much fun since it was in a bucket that would then get tossed outside when it needed to be, but in any regard, we hadn't been relying on people as the three square meals.

But, after all our patrolling, there are no answers, so we head back home. We chat about continuing to patrol as we've been doing. Every day, either Morgan or I will take one of the dogs and make a circuit of the lake and surrounding areas on foot, and we agree that Eve and Amy will begin joining those for fitness and experience. Neither of them have killed anything yet, but to Eve's point, we're a tiny group, and we'll all benefit from added firepower.

***

The next couple of weeks are dedicated to just that—teaching Amy and Eve how to fight. Morgan's exhaustive background in hand-to-hand combat techniques is invaluable, though watching her and Amy go through attacks, defensive moves, and so on is amusing. Morgan towers over the girl and outweighs her by thirty pounds, so it looks exactly like what it is—an early teenager fighting a full-grown, very fit, and stunningly fast adult. Eventually, Amy gets the basic hang of things to defend herself for a moment or two from simple assaults, but mostly, we work on the running away skill since the zombies aren't much faster than an easy jog and will usually lose interest once you get out of their direct line of sight. She accompanies us twice a day on the patrols, me in the mornings and Morgan in the afternoons, and proves to be nimble on her feet and a speedy runner whose endurance improves markedly to where I never have to stop and wait for her. Morgan will wear her out a bit more, but then again, Morgan will wear everyone out—in one way or another—and just keeps pushing her ever harder to ensure she can escape even a chase of a few miles without being too badly winded.

Eve's training is not as simple. She's no mean athlete, having been a top-notch golfer through college and into her early twenties, competing in regional tournaments and also keeping herself in good shape afterward at the gym in our old neighborhood. But Eve doesn't have a real mean streak. She's tough, physically and mentally, and won't quit a run or training session, not even the day when Morgan literally ran her into the ground to the point where Eve was throwing up on the side of the trail (but kept going). I saw her stand up to Morgan without fear when they first met, so I know she has a strong spine, too, but the killer instinct to finish a fight when it comes time to be ugly isn't there. She's a gentle, sensitive soul at her core.

That's great, except for … well … Morgan, who thrives in the new order. Her aggression and ferociously competitive nature now has no parameters when it comes to conflict, and I'd never seen someone fight with a smile on their face until we were across the lake, fighting the last batch of the invading zombies. She'd been grinning her way through the carnage and challenged me to a race back once the grisly work was done. She absolutely never quits, wanting to grind her opponent to miserable surrender in any contest; winning is nice, but making the other person or team quit in the process is *victory* in her mind. It doesn't make her a good sport exactly, but she was a world-class athlete in anything she'd put her mind to over the years and then, in the post-college years, a voracious fitness fanatic. So, she's the boss of hand-to-hand stuff.

I'm in charge of weapons-related training since I'm a better shot anyway—begrudgingly admitted by my sister—and also because someone being trained by Morgan shouldn't be allowed live ammunition in case they just decide to shoot her to get the endless prodding and pushing to cease. Amy turns out to be a decent enough marksman (markswoman? markskid?) with a small-caliber rifle we have, the one that had once been Amelie's. It's small enough so it doesn't startle her or twitch out of her hands when she fires, and just big enough so she can do some damage from a distance to a group. Eve doesn't like guns much, but we collectively convince her to become more adept with handguns and another rifle so she, too, can at least inflict injury to a distant group and handle herself for closer fighting. The ultimate, up-close, messy conflicts—where it gets down to sharp weapons and hands, elbows, and feet—are going to be where Morgan and I have to carry the group, but with our successful tour of the town, I hope we won't need any of this.

Morgan being Morgan, however, decides Eve should be her equal, or as close to it as possible. It doesn't go all that well. They're going through simple, nonweapons fighting, just showing Eve how to deflect an attack, how to duck under grasping arms, how to pivot and hit the attacker as they pass, and how to trip the other. For a while, it looks like shadowboxing, where no one's getting hit.

It's a fantastically clear and sunny day in the mid-70s, which is about right for this time of year. Outside the kitchen window is a narrow strip of land, perhaps twenty feet wide, that is covered with reluctant grass that needs to be cut maybe twice a summer, if at all. It's a good open space for this kind of work. Amy is inside napping after the morning patrol with me, and the dogs are lying contentedly in the dappled sunlight on the grass near where Morgan and Eve are working.

Both of the women are sweaty since they've been at it a while, and while I can tell Eve is tired, she isn't going to quit. Switching from defensive drills to offensive ones where Eve is the attacker, Morgan ducks under a half-hearted punch and slaps Eve across the face hard, like, twist-your-head hard. The blow echoes with a sharp *crack* across the smooth lake. Eve almost falls to the ground, catching her momentum with one hand, then righting herself, and I see she's seriously pissed. I watch closely but am so not going to get into the middle of this.

"Fuck you, Morgan!" she shouts. "What the hell was that?" Her hand flies up to the cheek that has been hit but then she clenches both of her fists and steps in close to my sister like she had when they first met. Morgan had driven the Corvette right past Eve, Ned, and Amy on the day all of them had arrived from Colorado and Pennsylvania, and Eve hadn't been too pleased at the time. Can't say I blame her.

Of course, Morgan never backs down from anyone, ever, so she happily stands her ground. "Do you want to, Eve? I could use some exercise of that kind. You at least could do something about it if you wanted to," she says with a nod in my direction.

I study the clouds. Well … there aren't any clouds, but I make sure to look thoroughly for them.

"Since there's not exactly a lot of options around here, I'd be willing to give you a try. Beats no action at all. Are you better at that than this? I hope so since if you throw bullshit punches, you're going to *die* in a real fight, not get slapped. What do you think is going to happen in a fight?" she continues, clearly fired up. "That a zombie or bad guy is going to give you a time-out because it's getting nasty? Because you're a *nice* girl? News flash, sunshine, they don't stop, ever. Ever! You know that, or you should by now. You fight, all in and until it's over and you win, or you die. It's as simple as that, and I'm trying to help you, dammit. That means I'm going to push you hard so that you're ready when you have to be ready. Grow up, Eve. You're not in Kansas anymore."

Eve strikes back, suddenly and fast enough that Morgan doesn't get to dodge or deflect the slap to her own face. It isn't a hard enough hit to move Morgan much, and she leans in to Eve and smiles. It's also possible she expected it and decided not to avoid it. "That's the spirit. Bring a little of that girl to the next fight, and maybe you'll be okay."

Eve spins on her heel and marches away around the house without looking at me, clearly fuming, probably a little embarrassed, and definitely not in need of company. Morgan looks over at me, grins, and shrugs. I'm not a huge fan of her methods, but I know she's right. You need to fully commit to the finish, whatever it takes to win, and nowadays, that includes killing. I want the girls to get along, but they don't have to be bosom buddies, especially since Morgan tends to alienate almost everyone sooner or later. But, Eve had fought back, so that's a good thing despite the bruised feelings and cheek. I think, aside from Morgan's constant prodding, challenging, and competitiveness, Eve mostly struggles with the new reality; she doesn't want to surrender to this rude, kill-or-be-killed world. While I can admire that, I also need her to be ready to finish the task when it's time, so I'm going to keep letting my sister do her thing.

It's a pretty darn quiet rest of the afternoon, even after Morgan takes off for her run/patrol with both dogs. Eve busies herself doing things that keep her away from the group, and when Amy attempts to go see what she's doing, I intercept her and suggest she give her some space. I know this is uncomfortable for Eve, but I also know she needs to work it out in her head at her own pace.

I can protect her ... but only so much.

***

Like always, we have a lot of chores to do, whether it's accumulating more firewood for the winter, finding additional food from grocery stores with amazingly short lines and nonexistent staff, working on shoring up the panic room beneath the floor of the cabin to be even more zombie proof, adding weapons to our armory, or doing general maintenance on the cabins. Those tasks take chunks out of our days but also allow for a lot of downtime. We swim in the lake, take the canoe or rowboat out—to the chagrin of the dogs, who are horrible passengers so are left on the shore to bark their fool heads off—walk around the shady path ringing the still waters of the lake that has been trod by many generations of many families, and play beanbag toss or darts in the driveway. We even have some spirited games of Wiffle ball across the lake in a sunny spot that has served as a field for ages.

Despite my attachment to the fond memories of youth and nostalgia for simpler times, there isn't a whole lot to really do here other than relax and find peace. Those are easy to relish over a long weekend as a child, but being here permanently is different. It's something of a limited and repetitive existence, and I feel some restlessness creeping into the group and think we need to mix things up.

On a clear and warm morning, we run the patrol and clean up after breakfast—oatmeal and blueberries and crappy instant coffee—then I suggest we go back toward town and play the golf course on the fringes. It probably isn't in great shape after a couple of years of neglect, but we'll have it to ourselves, and the greens fees will be reasonable. Morgan's a fantastic golfer who had worked as a teaching pro out west when she could behave herself, Eve is a college star, and I am ... well, I'm an okay golfer. My last round had been one of the best I've ever shot, even though no one had been watching to confirm my score, at least, aside from the crapload of zombies who interrupted the round from time to time. It didn't work out the way I'd planned at the time—I was searching for some kind of normal activity amid the sanity-testing days shortly after the infestation—but it had been a good change of pace. I met my first survivor on the back half of the course, a woman who was fleeing from a dozen or so of the monsters. While I'd been able to kill all of them in a bloody battle on the 12th fairway, she had been bitten herself in the process, and I was forced to make the horrible decision to kill her as well to keep myself safe. It was the first time I had come to the rude realization that hard decisions are a way of life now, like Morgan has been trying to get Eve to acknowledge. In hindsight, however, now having been bitten, and survived, I regret that decision even more than I had since maybe she wouldn't have turned. The guilt has followed me with the dogged intensity of a suburban woman hunting for pumpkin spice latte in the fall—never leaving my thoughts for too long, but there's nothing to be done about it now. And maybe I've just been lucky somehow. There isn't a good way to experiment on how people will react to being bitten and their survival rate.

Everyone's in for a change of pace and location, although Amy announces she won't be playing because golf is "stupid and boring," so she'll just come along since you don't leave the kids home alone anymore. We figure we'll be able to find clubs there at the course and anything else we really need, so we all get dressed and into the truck. There's a palpable energy in the cab as we creep out of the driveway, make our way down the dirt and gravel hill road to the main road, and turn right toward town.

Morgan and I had played the course when we were younger, a few times at least, until we got kicked off for threatening some of the regulars with bodily harm. We'd been in our late teens, and while Morgan was already a good golfer with a handful of years of experience, I held the game with a measure of disdain at the time because it wasn't physical enough, and I only reluctantly played a half-dozen times to that point. In other words, I stunk. When I'd slowed down and squared one up, the results were great. The problem was I did that about every 10th stroke, so I spent a lot of time trying to find my ball after it went howling into trees and scruff along the fairways.

Luckily, we'd been sent out in a gap between other groups, so the ones in front of us were gone from the first green by the time we teed up, and there was no one watching us hit our first balls either—which was good since there was nothing like having an audience to "settle" your nerves.

No problems for the first third of the round, but finally, the group behind us caught up, thanks to my wildness, and began to crowd us a bit. They were clearly ones who had been playing the course forever, played it quickly as some people were wont to do—sure, that four-foot putt is a gimme; go ahead and pick it up—and were put out by having to wait for young outsiders who were slowing them down. All four of them were somewhere in their early sixties, and there was nothing spectacular in their games. They were steady, down-the-middle players from what I'd seen, but they began to hit their shots close to us here and there, not waiting politely for us to find my ball and get back into the short grass. Then we heard the comments when they were parked and waiting for us to tee off, quiet at first but then obviously intended to be heard as they became more frustrated with the pace.

Morgan had been playing as well as always, so she wasn't the problem, but she *was* protective of me and began to bristle, mumbling under her breath each time we heard them, which started to interfere with her playing, and that really compounded things. It came to a head on the 10th tee, when they parked too close to the tee box to be considerate and bustled around their carts, making more noise than one should on the course. Morgan blasted off right down the middle of the fairway, curving her shot over the edge of a hill and trailing out of our line of sight, but I'd been thoroughly rattled by this time and howled a slicing drive off into the adjacent grazing pasture, narrowly missing a pair of cows.

"Hey, girlie, maybe you need to teach the boy the right way to do it," came the cackling comment, followed by laughter from the others. "He ain't got a clue about how to hit a golf ball, obviously. You all need to pick it up so we can maybe finish our round before it gets dark." It was all of eleven o'clock in the morning, and we were on the back nine already, so nightfall was not going to be a problem. He was just being a dick.

Morgan muttered, "Okay, that's it. I'm saying something. Those assholes could nicely ask to play through, but no, they've got to stay behind us so they can make shitty comments and fuck up your round. I'm done, and so are they."

"No, don't do anything, please, Morgan. Let's just tell them to go ahead. We can wait, and I don't want to get in trouble." I wasn't a wimp by any means, but I knew she was going to overdo it like she always did, and I wasn't in the mood for dealing with the fallout. But, once she was mad, there was no stopping her, so all I could do was watch and listen and hope we could wriggle out of whatever she was about to get us into.

She slid a 5-iron out of her bag, holding it like a baseball bat, rested it on her shoulder, and marched over to the heckler. He had no idea what was coming, but Morgan had already blossomed into a very attractive young woman, and I watched him ogle her rather than pay attention to her furious face. Lots of people made that mistake over the years, being distracted by her looks and not focusing on her body language. She stopped a half step from him, which was well inside normal personal space, but he had nowhere to go with the cart immediately behind him, so he leaned back as much as he could until the back of his head hit the frame of the roof. I strolled up too, holding my 3-wood down on the turf but making sure I had her back whether I wanted this to happen or not.

"Listen, you hick," she said, "everyone sucks at golf in the beginning, so get over yourselves and cut the crap. Shut your goddamn mouths or just ask to play through. You're hanging around and being assholes just for the sake of being assholes, and that stops now."

"Hey, boys, check this out. Little girlie here is telling us how to act on the golf course, *our* golf course. Isn't that somethin'?" He looked over his shoulder to his pals, none of whom had a club in their hands, and they chuckled in that way long-time golf course members do when faced with someone they consider beneath them. Plus, they outnumbered us, and they had never met Morgan. Mind you, this was a golf course in the middle-of-nowhere upstate New York, so it was hardly an exclusive place full of millionaire members. "Tell you what, girlie, how about the two of you kids just get yourselves off our course. We don't mind much lookin' at you play since those short shorts and tight shirt are showing your bits and pieces, but he's stinking up the place. We ain't got all day to wait around on you, so how's about you just git?" Another round of look-at-his-buddies-and-laugh-at-his-cleverness.

That was a mistake. A *big* mistake. I saw the tension build in Morgan's shoulders and thought she was going to hit him with the club right there, but she didn't, thank God. "Listen, grandpa. Turn your hearing aids up to eleven because I'm only going to warn you once. One more word, *one*, out of your mouth, and I'm going to hit you in the face with this club right here, and you can get yourself a whole new *full* set of teeth since I'm going to spray them all over the course. Who the hell do you think you are, acting like this? What's wrong with you? No, don't answer that since it'd be your one, and maybe last, word. The two of us could kill the four of you in about thirty seconds, bury your stupid, redneck bodies under the mound of cow shit over there, and be long gone before anyone knew anything was wrong. Shut your mouths, grab your damn clubs, hit your tee shots, and fuck off."

This was how she handled a lot of things. She just escalated it to where a reasonable person would never go, no messing around with negotiation. She just cut to crazy town, which scared the crap out of normal people, even jackasses like this who were absolutely unprepared for anything other than running their mouths. As objectionable as her methods were, they were also astonishingly effective since it was obvious she meant it.

His mouth opened as if to say something and hung there ajar for a moment before he wisely shut it. Most people with big mouths weren't prepared to back it up further and just yapped because, in most cases, they got away with it. These guys at least got the message that she was serious. Without making eye contact, he shuffled around the cart and grabbed a club, as did the others, and they went up to the tee box. Morgan, of course, wasn't going to let this happen peacefully and sounded off after each swing.

Golfer 1 (the mouth): Hurried swing, resulting in topping the ball not much farther than the women's tee box.

Morgan: "Thank goodness, you hit it past the ladies' tees. Would really, really hate to see that little old wrinkly dick make an appearance." In golfing parlance, when a male golfer didn't hit it past the ladies' tees, he was supposed to hang his dick out the front of his pants to prove his manhood. Always seemed like a stupid idea to me since I didn't need to see that, ever.

Golfer 2: Nervously peeked back at us a couple of times before hitting an okay-enough shot into the fairway and then hustled back to his cart.

Morgan: "Well, one of the big mouths can actually swing a golf club a bit, but I hit it farther than that when I was ten."

Golfer 3: Totally frazzled by all this, took a mighty swing that went over the top of the ball and missed it completely.

Morgan: "Oh, that was a practice swing, right? Didn't look like one. Looked more like one that was meant to hit the ball. You're going to add that to your score, right? Since swinging with intent counts as one."

He swung again and managed to hit the ball about 130 yards down the course, well off into the rough, and then darted sheepishly back to the cart as quickly as he could without looking up at us.

The last guy (Golfer 4) reluctantly made his way up, shoulders slumped, and was getting settled to swing when she piped up in the middle of his backswing. "Come on, princess, you can do it. You can hit it better than your inbred asshole buddies. Don't worry, I won't say anything after you hit it, so just relax!"

He might have been smarter than his pals since he shrugged his drooping shoulders and simply bent down, picked up his ball and tee, glanced at his tormentor, and walked away directly down the fairway instead of walking past us again to the carts. The two carts rattled to life and practically burned rubber down the path to escape. We stood and watched them hunt for their balls, hit their second shots after looking back at us—probably to make sure we weren't going to hit at them—and waited for them to finish the hole and drive away from the green before continuing our own round.

"Shame we'd already hit our balls. I would've liked to whistle one right through them before that second shot," Morgan said with a triumphant look on her face. "Well, that was fun. I bet the rest of their round sucks, which is great. Okay, let's play golf."

I shook my head at all of this, but I'd been angry myself with the quick trigger of youth and the insult to her, so I was fine with the outcome if not the method.

We finished our round without further ado and enjoyed the course to ourselves until we got back to the clubhouse. We were met by an angry manager and our even angrier grandfather, who had clearly been called about the ruckus and was mortified by Morgan's behavior. It was a small town after all, and a lot of people had been there forever and knew one another well. He wordlessly escorted us over to the cars, and once there, he informed us that we weren't welcome to play the course ever again, scolding Morgan for terrorizing men he'd known for decades. She just laughed and got in the car. I kept my mouth shut. My sister, ladies and gentlemen.

But now, no one's there to tell us no, so we're going to play. The clubhouse, such as it is, is unlocked, and we browse through all the inventory to choose clubs, balls, shoes, the works. If we're going to play, may as well outfit ourselves properly. Luckily, there are pull carts, so we don't have to haul our clubs by hand; it's a hilly course, and compromising our hands is a bad strategy. Amy, at last, finds a visor she thinks is cool, and once we're ready, we walk over to the first tee.

The grass is scruffy and overgrown like I'd expected, but since the growing season here is shorter than elsewhere, it isn't too bad. Maybe if this becomes a habit, I can learn how to run all the huge mowers in the utility shed as well as the specialized ones for the greens. It will certainly give us something to do from time to time. I know I respond well to having tasks to accomplish, so even if I have to come solo, I know this will give me some contentment.

After tossing a tee into the air to decide who's going to hit first—whichever person the pointy end lands facing gets the honors, kind of like spin the bottle, now that I think of it—I turn out to be the "winner." Awesome. I'm the least accomplished of the golfers and always get a bit of nerves on the first tee for no good reason since I'm a solid, if unspectacular, player now. I do, however, have a lot fewer reps under my belt than Morgan and Eve, so I take my time getting ready. Not that the first shot sets the tone for the round exactly, but it never hurts to get off to a good start.

Which I do.

The first hole is a low, downhill par 3 of about 230 to 240 yards, so I don't need to hit driver or even 3-wood. I get along fairly well with my 4-iron back home and don't want to hit any more than right around 200 yards since the ball will trickle onto the green if you get it right. Landing on the green itself is a bad idea; it slopes away from the tee boxes, and the ball will merrily roll right off the back.

I hammer the ball right down the fairway, cutting it in half as neatly as you please, and watch as it carries just beyond about 200 yards, bounces a couple of times, and stops. I grin, mostly to myself since I know I'm not going to win today, and step back just as both Ajax and Jack tear off down the course. We watch the two magnificent dogs race down the hill, across the green carpet of the fairway, and toward the green. My ball has come to a rest just a foot shy of the shorter grass, and dammit if those two fools aren't playing fetch. Ajax somehow beats the longer-legged shepherd there and happily scoops my ball up and trots back to drop it at my feet with a doggy grin.

"Bad dog!" I say, though I really don't mean it.

Since he doesn't understand human, he ignores me and sits to watch Eve hit next, haunches bunched beneath him to chase her shot down. However, she simply looks at the dogs, firmly says, "No," and hits her own shot. The dogs stay still as she smoothly swings with her 3-wood, and we all follow the flight of the ball until it lands just past where mine had, bounces high, and spills onto the green about 10 yards from where the flag is standing in the back left corner.

"Nice shot!" I'm surprised at this coming from Morgan, who's spare with compliments and horribly competitive, and since we know this course, I can tell she's expecting to wipe the floor with both Eve and me. She, too, strolls to hit, also pausing to tell the dogs "No," and hits her own shot. Almost an identical outcome to Eve's, but her ball is a foot or two closer to the pin. I know I'm outmatched, but this is a little ridiculous.

"Are you going to hit another one?" Morgan asks me.

"What do you mean? We all saw where my shot went before the two furry dipshits picked it up. I'm going to drop mine right where it was."

"I don't know what you're talking about. All I see are two balls on the green, and those are mine and Eve's. I think you need to hit." She's smiling broadly as she needles me, no differently than she has our entire lives, and I know this trip was a really good idea. Competition brings out the best (and worst) in my sister, and taking some time out from routine has been one of my better plans.

"Kiss my ass. I'm invoking the 'stupid dog drop rule,' and I get to hit first since I'm away. Watch and learn, smarty-pants, maybe you'll pick up some tips." No way am I going to win, but a little lively smack talk is appropriate.

Eve watches all this back-and-forth without a word, and I have a feeling she's calculating her odds against Morgan. After all, she's highly competitive, too, and golf is her game, so this should be interesting.

We all laugh and walk down to the green together, trailing our hand carts complete with shotguns and rifles. Amy is in charge of the score and has a pencil and scorecard tucked into her shorts' front pocket. This time, I'm not going to play with the .45 in my waistband since I'm not alone, but despite our merriment, we all instinctively scan the views for both the right golf shot to make and any threats that would require a different kind of shot. We're more relaxed than we have been for a while, confident they brought their whole army last time, and we dispatched every single one of them.

I miss my shot, rolling my chip just past the cup, but I'm content with a tap-in par on the first hole. Both of the women leave their putts short, probably due to the green being slower than it would be if it had been consistently maintained, so their muscle memory had told them something different than their eyes should have, and they tapped in for par as well. One down, all even for scores, and no zombies. Good stuff.

The second hole is uphill and over 400 yards, so a par 4. Back at the clubhouse, I found the same model driver I'd used most recently to hit well through my last North Carolina round until using it to beat a zombie to re-death on the 18th hole. I'm looking forward to using this one since I gained some good distance off the tee with it, and since I'm still going first, thanks to our identical scores, I step into the tee box and—wait for it, this is a shocker, folks—predictably overswing by a ton. All golfers have a tendency to do that anyway when faced with an uphill hole, even though all golfers know better, and it's going to take at least two shots to reach the green, but human nature is what it is. It's great contact, and I utterly mash the ball, but it starts to slice hard to the right almost immediately and crosses over the rough, over the entry road that borders the course, and into an undeveloped field on the opposite side.

"Shit," I mutter and then remember I hadn't told the dogs no before hitting. I look hopefully at them, expecting a race to the ball again. Nope. Ajax swivels his head toward mine but stays dutifully put. Dammit. "So you two morons chase after the perfect drive but leave the banana slice alone, and I get to go fetch it? Ungrateful furballs. No snacks for you later, leaving me hanging like this. I'm going to read up on neutering, too, when we get back home."

The ladies hit, both of them into the middle of the fairway, no problems, and we all march away, just me off at a tangent to try and find my wayward ball. The next handful of holes are similar. I'm either good or terrible off the tee, the dogs ignore my bad shots and chase my good ones, even when I tell them not to, and the two women are playing to a draw thus far. I find myself more observing their dynamic than concentrating on my own round, liking the way Eve focuses on her shots and then swings beautifully with little visible effort. Morgan is different. Her game is less elegant and more athletic, where her raw physical power gives her more distance than Eve, while Eve's touch around the green is finer than Morgan's. They stay dead even for score through the first fourteen holes, and I trail them by eight strokes, which I consider something of a victory.

The 15th hole is a downhill par 5, which is one of my favorites since hitting downhill makes you look like a hero, as the ball will stay in the air forever. It also faces back into the valley and vaguely in the direction of town, across farmland in various shades of green and dotted with houses. A pretty view. The ladies hit first, and as I'm getting ready to go, I sense Ajax tighten up. He stands with the burble of a growl in his throat, staring in the same direction as the hole, with the hackles on his back beginning to stand up. I can't see anything. "Easy, boy, nothing to be freaked out about. I'm not going to do anything bad here, though if I do, it'd be nice to get an assist for a change."

He doesn't move, and I still don't see anything other than the lovely green vista stretching off into the distance, so I go ahead and set up to hit.

"Oh!" Amy's gasp brings me to a halt in the middle of my backswing, and I look over at her.

She's staring off in the same direction as the dog had, and her younger eyes have found what ours didn't. Now, way out at the edge of my vision, I see the shape of a person moving toward us. It moves at a slow pace and unsteadily, so we all immediately think it's a zombie and drop our golf stuff to pick up our gunpowder stuff. No reason for us to do anything impetuous; we have the great line of sight and the high ground, and we stack the golf bags in front of us and the hand carts behind that, as something of an abatis.

I have the rifle with a scope, so I slide that out of my golf bag, settle myself flat on the downy grass, rest the gun on the bag, and sight until I have the figure centered in the reticle. I watch carefully for a moment, move the gun from side to side, scanning for anything else of note, and then lift my head up. "It's a human, a man. I can't see anything or anyone else. Something is wrong with him, maybe he's injured or very old because he's not moving in a straight line, and his clothes are a mess. Another survivor, I think. Let's go get him. Morgan, you stay here with Amy and Jack. I'll leave this rifle with you so you can be on overwatch. Let me have your shotgun. Eve, Ajax, and I will go down there and check him out. If something goes haywire, we'll run and meet you at the abandoned barn over by where the main road turns into the course driveway." I toss her the keys to the truck.

Everyone nods in agreement, though the fun of the afternoon has fled off into the distance like one of my errant tee shots. We haven't seen any humans up here since the run-in with the three men very early on after arriving, and then Top's addition to our group at the same time. I think back to our recent trip through town, when we'd been honking the horn on the truck and trying to find anything living (or dead) still there, and it was silent. He came from somewhere, and from the looks of him through the scope, he's been walking a long distance and is worn out. We'll find out soon enough.

Eve and I finish arming ourselves and move off downhill, Ajax at Eve's heel as we split up and flank the man resolutely making his unsteady way toward us. As we get closer, I'm able to see more clearly and can tell he's somewhere well on the high side of fifty and terribly thin, his clothes hanging off bony shoulders like the bedraggled rags of an abandoned scarecrow that's seen too many northeastern winters. More than once, he stumbles and falls, wearily standing back up and continuing his trudging, meandering pace. He has obviously seen us; there's no other reason for him to be coming in this direction, and he finally offers a weak, faltering wave as we close to within 100 yards. He then drops to the ground and doesn't rise.

I motion to Eve to stay alert, glance back uphill to the silhouettes of Morgan and Amy, and rush over to kneel next to him. I'm right, he's older and barely more than a skeleton. It makes me think this is what the Allied soldiers must have seen as they reached the concentration camps at the end of World War II and found those few, "lucky" survivors. He stinks with the reek of someone unbathed for months—not that we're all roses, but we at least take near-daily baths in the lake—and his skin stretches taut across every bone that's visible, pulling sharply against his cheekbones and forehead. Mostly bald on top, long unkempt flaps of hair hang over his ears, and he has a scruffy beard dotted heavily with gray draping down to hide his neck, and the flannel shirt he's wearing looks three sizes too big for him.

Eve gasps as she moves in closer, holding her hand over her mouth and nose, and Ajax sniffs once and then moves away. The poor man is close to death, that much is obvious, but he has made some effort to reach us, and I'm anxious to understand why. I sweep his sweaty hair away from his face as he lies on the ground with his eyes closed for a minute, and I'm startled when he opens them to display fierce, green eyes that burn with clarity and perhaps a little madness.

"Monsters!" he shouts. "Monsters! The monsters, they're gone!"

A hacking cough interrupts whatever he meant to say next, and I prop him up a bit to clear his throat. "Yes, you're safe, there are no monsters here, just people." The odor pouring off him makes my own eyes water; his breath is a fetid reek of God knows what, and I unconsciously move my head away from him.

"They came for us! All of us! They found us all and took us to the room. Trapped! Trapped for months. Dead, all dead but me. Alone. Hungry." He moans, looking at me but not really seeing me in clear focus, just staring wildly around in panic. Tears flow from the corners of those brilliant eyes, clearing tracks in the grime that covers his face as they wander.

I have no idea what he's talking about other than it sounds similar to what happened with Eve and DeeDee back in North Carolina. After months on the run and in hiding, they were eventually caught and delivered to me by the zombies who had started systematic searches directed by the alpha zombie. "Sir, you're okay now, we're not monsters." I speak as soothingly as I can, trying to calm him down if possible. "We killed all of them not too long ago. They're gone. Can you tell me what you're talking about? Are there others that we can go find and help?"

He finally makes eye contact with me and takes an alarmingly shuddering breath. "The room … they're in the room. All of them."

"What room? Where is it?"

He coughs heavily once, then again, spraying a mix of blood and spit onto his beard as he does so, and I feel his body sink. He's going, that much is clear, but even though he said he was alone, if there is a chance there are other survivors trapped somewhere, I need to find out. I can hear Eve sobbing softly behind me.

"What room?" I repeat. "How can we help the others? Are there others?"

What little weight he still has sags even more heavily in my arms, and I think he's gone, so I gently shake him, anxious to hear the rest. Nothing at first, and he closes his eyes, chin drooping toward his thin chest with a dribble of phlegmy blood spilling onto his shirt. His breathing slows.

"The grocery ... the back ..." he whispers. Then one more shout. "Monsters!" And he's gone.

I let him go and gently lie him back onto the grassy turf. Eve comes over and rests a hand on my shoulder; I look up to see tears pouring down her anguished face. I just shake my head and stand up. We have work to do, and if this sad soul's condition is anything of an indicator, we need to hurry and find the others he talked about. There's only one grocery store in the town, and while we searched the public areas and collected food and water there during our last trip, we didn't go into the storage spaces. We have no clue what we're about to discover, but it will lead us to everything else.

CHAPTER 4

We wave the rest of the group down to join us and catch them up. The four of us collect rocks from the nearby retaining wall, cover the body, and say something of a eulogy, asking for peace. It's a tall order these days, but I hope he's gone to somewhere better than whatever he'd escaped from. We trudge silently back uphill to collect our things, though drop all the golf gear back inside the clubhouse since there's no need to take it with us, and no one's going to disturb it until our next round, if there is one. Our previously light mood is officially gone.

It's now getting late in the afternoon, and we prefer to be home before nightfall, always. While we're pretty confident we got them all, nothing says more haven't arrived, so caution is the word of the day, every day. But there's no way we can't go back into town to see if there are others we can rescue. We have powerful flashlights in the truck and are fully armed as always, so we agree to take the chance as the sun drifts lower to the western horizon.

The town is quiet, which is expected, and shadows from the hills and houses to the west drape long across the empty streets while the facades across the street are bathed in the yellow blare of late-day sunlight. I drive slowly, taking any warning of "monsters" seriously, and the rest of the group scan in all directions, looking for signs of trouble. The dogs are alert in the back but not alarmed, just looking around with their tongues lolling. We reach the grocery store in short order and stop out front, staring at the now-ominous entry doors for a moment before shutting down the truck and climbing out.

I'm thinking we aren't likely to find anything dangerous here but am hesitant to bring anyone else inside with me. Morgan and I always split up if we segregate the group, leaving one physical person with one less so, but I don't want Amy or Eve in jeopardy in an enclosed space, so I decide to take just the dogs with me. They aren't likely to get upset by anything, and if for some reason, we run into a fight, we'll all be okay enough. The women all come to the threshold of the store and watch while I shove the now not-automatic doors open and step into the dark building. My usual preference is the shotgun since it does incredible damage, especially in tight spaces, but since I need a free hand for the flashlight, I only carry the .45 handgun this time.

Ajax is on my left and Jack on my right as I go down the cereal aisle, the light from the torch cutting into the deepening shadows of the farthest reaches of the store. It's totally silent indoors, which still takes some getting used to—no whirring of refrigeration, clattering of carts, beeping of registers, or murmuring of shoppers. Just quiet, like all stores these days.

I stop as the light finds the aluminum double-swing doors that lead into the rear storage sections, and I pick up an unsettling smell. My heart rate rises, and I watch the dogs carefully since they're our furry alarm systems. The two of them stand still with no indication they've picked up anything of concern, so I move ahead and shove through the left-hand door and wedge it open with a folded scrap of cardboard torn from a nearby box. If I have to run, I want to keep a clean escape route and line of sight.

The smell is stronger now, and I have an uneasy feeling growing. There's little natural light probing into these back rooms. A scant handful of small windows near the ceiling allow the fading day in, but it's almost full dark, and I wish the power were on. I make my way farther back and finally come to the door of what must have been the refrigerated or frozen storage. It's a solid aluminum door about four feet wide and eight feet tall, and it hangs slightly ajar.

Your door is ajar! No, your door is a door. What's behind Door Number Two, I wonder?

What the fuck is that smell? Are you feeling lucky?

No, not really.

I make the dogs sit and tell them to stay while I step forward. With my gun in hand, I slowly edge the door open with the butt, holding the flashlight waist-high as I do so. The horrible smell washes over me, and it's all I could do to not turn my head away in disgust. After a couple of seconds, I have no choice.

There have been many unbearable moments since the dawn of the zombies, but this is the worst. Corpses litter

the entire space, piled haphazardly on top of one another, large and small, young and old, intermingled in a horrifying puzzle of death. I choke on the waves of reek that climb over me and throw up violently onto my shoes. I can't hold the flashlight steady for more than a few seconds at a time, but it illuminates faces, arms, and legs, all of them dead and in various stages of both decomposition and having been devoured. I've never been a horror movie fan at any point in my life, not liking the monster-jumping-out-from-the-shadows moments nor the gore nor the flickering techniques that had become popular to show the carnage the director had dreamt up. This is worse, *so* much worse since they're real people, or had been, and my flashlight lights up tiny vignettes of misery everywhere it goes. A face twisted in silent agony, arms draped over their neighbor—perhaps reaching for comfort, a child's open eyes staring at nothing. I try to steel myself and take a thorough look, but I just can't take it. There isn't anything good here. And the smell: a horrid cocktail of unwashed bodies, effluence, pain, fear, and desperation. I stagger back, weeping and fighting the urge to vomit again, and race back out into the main shopping areas to try and compose myself.

They were stored like animals, like chattel. This answers how the zombies had survived the winter. They'd collected all the people and crowded them into that compact space to be eaten as needed. My mind bends at the thought.

Hey, you guys killed the zombies a few weeks back. That guy you found, what do you think he's been up to since then? People can't live for too long without food, you know.

No. I'm not going down that road. I shut the voice out.

I stumble back through the aisles toward the three flashlight beams waiting for me outside and hopefully toward a tighter grasp on sanity. Wordlessly, I get into the truck, and after a quizzical moment among the women, they get in too.

"What did you find?" I don't even know who asks this.

"Nothing. There wasn't anything there for us. Let's go home."

Morgan goes to speak, but I just look at her and shake my head a bit, and she closes her mouth. We drive home, and I go right for the whiskey, sitting alone and in silence on the front porch for a long, long time and staring into the night for answers. What did this? What broke the world?

CHAPTER 5

I don't find that answer in the darkness but rather fall asleep on the lounger again. At least there's no duct tape or snake this time. I awake the next morning to find Eve and Morgan creeping out of the front door. My head aches, but it's difficult to tell if that's from what looks like a prodigious amount of booze consumed, based on the near-empty bottle next to me, or the images that are never, ever going to leave my mind. Thankfully, the voice inside is remaining quiet for now.

Eve starts the conversation smartly by handing me a huge steaming mug of coffee and giving me a moment to drink some. "What did you see?"

"Nothing I ever want to see again. It was the people from the town, not all of them, but whatever the zombies must have decided was enough to get them through the cold weather. He was right. They were trapped, and all of them were dead." Pictures flicker, and I try hard to dodge them.

"I'm sorry."

"So am I. I don't know what I think is worse, the part where the zombies were again smarter than we expected, or the idea of being in their position, of being trapped and terrified. Whatever caused all of this, if it was a person's fault, there isn't a punishment that's harsh enough for all of the shit we've been through. And we're the fortunate ones since we're still upright."

Morgan jumps in quickly. "Yes, you're right, we are the fortunate ones, and we have to do what we can to help other people. That's why we have to go to Kansas City and get those people out of there. Eve and I have been talking this morning, and she agrees. Think about what we have here now. Food, water, safety, more than enough room for us, good people but not enough people. There are only the four of us, and that's dangerous. We've been lucky."

I've kind of known that this was going to come up. Not today, necessarily, but at some point. Morgan isn't a good one for unfinished business nor for being outmaneuvered like she was when she'd stopped at that suburban fortress on her way here. There had been a clutch of houses joined by cinder-block walls to form a two-story perimeter wall where a few dozen people were surviving and being led by a charismatic but sadistic man named Marcus. He and a few minions held them there by fear and the offering of security in this wonderful new world but extracted "tribute" from the females in the group every month. Morgan just got lunch and supplies, but she was there long enough to speak to one of the trapped women, find out the details, and try to get some of those people to join her when she continued her journey. That didn't work out, and all she'd gained from the stop was Jack the dog and a healthy dose of pissed off.

"I agree we have something good to offer, but you just made the key point. There are only four of us, and, really, only three of us can handle a fight, and that's being generous. No offense, Eve, but I'm not sure you're ready to pull the trigger. Even with the dogs, we've got shitty odds, and people are a lot smarter and less predictable than zombies. I don't know if I can get on board. We'd be risking our own safety for complete strangers." I doubt I'm going to win this argument, but I want to make sure we're looking at the big picture versus the Morgan-is-still-angry one since I've had *lots* of practice with that over the decades.

Morgan's face shifts to an expression I haven't seen in a long time: sadness, though spiced with a smidge of angry. "I'm going, with or without the rest of you. What we just discovered, people trapped and hopeless and scared, I can't let that go without trying. It reminds me too much of that time," she says plaintively as she makes eye contact with me.

Ah, that time. Not as good a story as the other "that time" with the girls tying me up. Some memories are willing ones that stick around to nicely come for a visit, others drift in the space of your head and elude you like a feather on a windy day. Some, like what I just saw last night, are ones you work hard to chase away. This is one of those for me, though it was a far less harrowing night for me than for Morgan.

***

She's a sophomore in college, and I'm a high school junior. My sister's, um, powerful personality has been in place since before she was ten years old, never backing down from a challenge, zero fear, and as a consequence, she's jumped into a bunch of scrapes over the years. I frequently got dragged into those, but our credo was and is pretty simple. We have each other's back, period. I've had her back a lot more than she's had mine, and as a result, I bore many bumps, bruises, and scars to commemorate the impetuosity of my sister.

Either our parents had wanted a weekend on their own, or they'd utterly lost their minds, but they allowed me to drive to visit her at school. Like any big-college-campus students, hers know how to party on the weekends—not that the weeknights are timid, exactly—and she brings me to a party at the football frat house.

Morgan is already wildly popular and knows a ton of people, thanks to her volleyball prowess and looks, not to mention her all-in approach to life. If life was a car, hers had no brake pedal, and followers always swarmed to her, so she was rarely alone. Tonight, however, she decides to ditch the crowd and hang out with her little brother, which means a lot to me.

We get to the party, where the cavemen at the front door hold up cardboard pieces with numbers on them, ranking the newest entrants on a scale of 1 to 10. Morgan gets a standing ovation and a 10, thanks to her sleeveless shirt with a plunging neckline and short shorts I wished she hadn't worn, and I get some hoots of derision because I'm carrying my pool cue in a tiny case.

The chip on Morgan's shoulder extends to knocking down pompous assholes. She told me to bring it when I visit because this specific frat has a guy who brags about his pool-playing prowess nonstop, and she wants me to cut him down a few pegs. Our family had gotten a pool table in the basement when I was no more than seven years old, and Dad had gathered a handful of milk crates for me to stand on and cut down a cue to my size. I took to the game quickly and played endlessly throughout my teenage years, finding solace in the solitude of practice while playing music. It helped me through the typical breakups and other assorted growing-up bullshit. By the time I go to visit her, there isn't a shot I haven't seen or made, and I'm nearly equally adept at playing both left- and right-handed. I've set people up by playing them lefty for a few games, letting them think they have a chance, and then swap over to my right hand and wipe them out quickly. My sister and I made a good bit of money over the most recent winter, on a family ski trip, when the two of us had gone to a bowling alley at night that had tables, and I hustled a few locals out of about one hundred dollars before it got ugly and we had to run for the door. So basically, I'm good, damn good, and she wants to both show off her little brother and settle down the loudmouth.

We wind our way through the writhing clutches of drunk college kids, who're studying diligently and making good use of their parents' money, to the room where the table is set up next to a long wooden bar scarred by decades of abuse, with the keg taps facing out for self-service. Morgan grabs a couple of beers for us, which is a bit of a novelty for me, but I act like I have them all the time, and we lean back against the bar to scout things out. The guy she told me about, Adam, is holding court and beating everyone who plays him.

Morgan chats aimlessly with nearby drunks, and I watch him play, sipping my beer and surreptitiously looking for his weak spot. He's good, too, and I notice he isn't drinking much, so he dispatches his hammered challengers without much work.

After a handful of games, I pick up that he lets his confidence get in the way of his focus. He's probably been beating these same people easily for years, and as a result, he doesn't hone in on every shot and leaves some simple ones unmade just out of laziness. I don't have that problem. When I'm playing, I completely tune out the world and grind into the details of how hard to hit, where is my next shot (or shots), and where will my leave be, and I have a superb touch for finesse shots. On a good day, I'll break, drop a couple of balls there, and, about half the time, run the table without letting my opponent even take a shot.

"You got him?" Morgan asks, turning away from a guy leaning toward her much more closely than I like.

"Yeah. He's pretty good, but I'll win. What do you have in mind?"

"Lefty first? Or just wipe him out?"

"I don't know … he might be good enough to beat me lefty. He's not drinking either, so he won't be sloppy. He's just a bit lazy."

"Tell you what, I've got this."

With that, she pushes herself off the bar, saunters over to him through the crowd, and speaks in his ear. I can't hear over the music and hubbub, but every time she says, "I've got this," I'm usually sorry later, so I figure she's cooking something up. She doesn't disappoint.

After a minute of the two of them talking and glancing over at me, they both walk over. "This is Adam," Morgan says. "I told him you could beat him at pool, and that even though you brought your own cue, you wouldn't use it, just a house stick."

Adam is a good four inches taller and fifty pounds bigger than me, and he stands over me inside my personal space, smirking as only a career jock can do.

Awesome, Morgan. Thanks.

I'm not intimidated, just annoyed with her since I'm sure the pool cues in a fraternity house are about as good as broomsticks. "Hey," I say, introducing myself and holding my hand out. "Nice to meet you."

"Whatever, you little douchebag. What are you, twelve?" he practically shouts with his big mouth, so everyone within twenty feet can hear him even over the throbbing music.

And so, we get off on the right foot, pals for life. I'm a three-sport athlete and gym rat myself, and I definitely don't look twelve, but I'm still a kid by comparison. I feel anger flare and know I've turned red, but the dim lighting will hide that. I'm going to embarrass this gorilla in front of all his friends. No lefty-to-righty switch, just a beat down.

Placing my cue in its cover behind the bar, I go over and find an okay-enough cue on the wall rack and chalk it up—and I'm happy there's chalk. I gesture for him to break, and he does so with a thunderous *crack*, sinking one ball and then continuing his turn. He sinks three more before missing and steps back from the table proudly. "Go ahead, kid. I've only got three left before the 8 ball. Good luck, but you're screwed. Nobody in this whole school beats me."

Yeah, uh-huh, I think as I ready for my turn. I scan the table, see my first five shots will be easy enough, and glance over at Morgan, who's returned to the bar and is watching over the rim of her beer. She winks at me in a dorky-for-her way. I step to the table without a word and quickly sink those five balls, dropping them right in the center of the pockets and leaving the next shot lined up well each time. I see I can finish the next two and then the 8 ball, but I decide to have a little fun with him.

Missing my next shot on purpose, though not obviously, I leave the cue ball against the rail, trapped by one of my balls. He has zero chance of making any of his. Most people play where you have to hit your own ball first, or your turn is over, but he leans over the ball, clearly hits mine first, and sinks one of his remaining three balls in with the illegal combination shot.

That's fine, I think, *my turn now.* I move toward the table and grab the chalk.

"What do you think you're doing? It's still my shot unless you're blind. I sunk my ball. Back the fuck up, junior."

I hesitate, even opening my mouth to protest for a second, and then shut it as I make eye contact with my sister. She shakes her head, just a bit, so I simply nod and step back. "My bad. Didn't know the house rules."

Adam finishes the table and looks up smugly as the 8 ball drops in the corner pocket. Not at me, but at Morgan. "Your kid brother isn't a total bag of shit, but that wasn't even hard. I'm going to beat him like we beat State last weekend, all night until he gives up and takes his little pool cue home to Mommy."

Morgan simply smiles, digs into the front pocket of her shorts, pulls out a folded twenty-dollar bill, and tosses it onto the table. "How about you put your money where your mouth is?"

He looks at the bill, then at her, then at me, then pulls a fairly fat money clip out and flips a twenty-dollar bill of his own onto the felt next to hers. "You bet your ass, honey. And when you and him lose, we'll come up with something else for payment on top of the cash."

"Whatever, just play," she snaps back. She shoots me a scowl, letting me know she knows I missed on purpose and shouldn't screw around anymore.

When I finish racking the balls, Adam shoves me out of the way as he moves back to the head of the table. "My break since I won." Another *crack* as he leans into the break. One of the tricks of the trade is to subtly leave the balls just a little loose in the rack for someone who sets up to break from an off-center position. In a dim room, it's impossible to see, and most people don't know to look for it anyway. I do and watched where he broke from the first time. Details and focus.

While he mashes the shot, the balls scatter nicely but without anything falling. "Shit! Nothing."

I don't say anything again, just study the way the balls are arrayed, figure out the sequence, and then go to work.

No fooling around this time; I've learned that lesson. I move quickly, sinking all my striped balls and then the 8 without missing, and scoop the two twenties up off the end of the table. There isn't much that's more annoying than being unable to even take a turn, and I know we'll be playing again before he even says it. What he isn't doing is thinking. He knows he won the first game only by cheating, and now I've just run the table with little effort, which means I'm very good. It's just that his ego has been dinged by a high schooler in front of his teammates and friends, so he wants another chance.

"Double or nothing." Not a question. He extracts the money clip again and flicks a pair of twenties out onto the deep green felt.

"No problem. Losers rack, like you said."

He stares at me for a second, but then he goes to the far end of the table and racks the balls quickly. I watch carefully since there's a solution for almost everything on a pool table, and adjust the cue ball to be centered on the opposing dot. He racks loose just to be a dick, not out of strategy like I had, knowing I can't protest in "his" house.

Morgan grins at me through a gathering crowd and turns to talk to another football player. She knows I have this, so while she's going to stay nearby, there isn't much need to watch what's going to happen too closely. I suppress a smirk of my own, lean over, and break. Two balls drop, both stripes, and the humiliation commences. I run that table, too, without missing, and the next. The big fellow is practically steaming since he's lost three games in a row without taking a shot, and twenty, forty, and eighty dollars in succession since he kept being stupid enough to keep suggesting (demanding) double or nothing. Anyone with a brain would decide that losing one hundred forty bucks is enough, and the other guy is too good to mess with, but maybe he's had enough beer to think he's going to win it back. I almost feel bad for him. Almost.

"Hey, Jimmy," he says to a nearby dark-haired guy wearing a red jersey. "Give me some cash for a minute. I'm out, and I need to play again. I'm going to kick his ass this time."

Jimmy hesitates but then hands over a wad of cash. I know these are all rich kids, but this is a bit nuts. I'm up more money in an hour than I make in a month working my job in the mall food court making cheesesteaks, and he's about to drop more on the table. And it's still my break. And I'm red-hot.

"Okay, kid. Double or nothing. A hundred and sixty if you have the balls for it. My break too. House rules are three games max."

I doubt that anyone, ever, has run the table three times in a row here. He just made the rule up on the spot. I don't like it, but there isn't anything I can do. This is their turf, and a few more football players have drifted over to watch the action. I don't see Morgan anywhere, but there isn't anything she can do either. I shrug and move to the side and then down to rack the balls. Loose again, just a hair, since he still sets up in the same spot.

There's no guarantee, of course, that he'll miss. Like anything else, it's an improvement in the odds, and this time, he sinks a ball on the break. "Now, it's Adam's turn," he crows. He sinks three more balls but then misses and leaves me a tough shot, but otherwise good table. I make the bank shot without blinking for the first ball and then run the table again, making one mistake, which is due to the hubris of a young ego.

When lining up the last shot, I'm at the opposite corner from where Adam stands with a furious expression on his face. I have an easy, straight shot to make for the 8 ball, and after setting my hands, I look up and away from the table to make eye contact with him. "You know, you were right. No one in this school beats you at pool. It took a kid in *high school* to beat you." I never lose eye contact as I say this, and smoothly shoot the final ball in without looking back down at it. Cocky? Yes, indeed. Maybe a little dumb, too, but teenage boys are good at both of those.

I walk slowly down to the pile of cash on the table and sweep three hundred twenty dollars up carefully, stuff it into the pocket of my jeans, and set the pool cue back in the rack on the wall. There isn't anything left to prove, and I doubt anyone is going to loan him more cash. This is a losing proposition, and everyone here knows it, no matter how drunk they are.

People are whispering behind their hands to each other, looking at a very red-faced Adam, and giggling. I can see he's furious, and it's only then I fully realize this may not have been a good idea and look around for Morgan. If I'm going to get in a fight with one or more of these monsters, thanks to her setting me up, I'm sure going to drag her into it. I still don't see her anywhere, and Adam is forcing his way around the table, through the very interested crowd, toward me, scowling and flexing.

Uh-oh.

Just as he's about to reach me, he's intercepted by Jimmy, who places a restraining hand on his chest and speaks in his ear. Adam keeps staring at me, shakes his head a couple of times, but then finally nods and swings around to move back through the crowd with one last angry look over his shoulder. Jimmy trails behind him without looking at me.

You just got damn lucky. A smart kid would find his sister and get the fuck out of here. Like, now.

Very true.

I look around the room, scanning for Morgan, but still no luck. The ground floor of the frat house has a good handful of rooms, and while this is the biggest one since it has to accommodate the pool table and bar, plus swarms of college kids, it's in the back of the house. I figure she's in one of the front rooms, so I collect my cue from behind the bar and start to make my way back out.

I'm intercepted by boobs. I mean, by a girl. Well, a girl with boobs, and those boobs are well displayed in some kind of silky green tank top, a low-cut thing that makes it really obvious she isn't wearing a bra since I can see more than half of her chest. I'm sixteen. Actual three-dimensional boobs, not ones on the internet or in a magazine, are the promised land, and I freeze.

It takes a second or two (or five), but I finally look up to find a cute redhead who reminds me of Cassie from what feels like so long ago, looking at me with a smile on her face. Green eyes to match her blouse flutter at me below soft curls of hair falling loose from whatever contraption girls use to pull their hair up. She leans in to speak to me, displaying even more skin in the process, and brings her mouth close to my ear. Her breath smells like beer and pot. "Hi! I'm Katherine. That was awesome, you beating Adam like that. He's an asshole. Want to get a drink?"

She's a little unsteady on her heels, and I admit that, at that age, I'm immediately not thinking about much other than my chances of getting very naked with Katherine as soon as possible. If beer leads to naked, I'm all for beer. Despite my limited experience with anything beyond fumbling my way around the general location of third base a few times, and still being a bit nervous around girls and with the subject in general, I'm very interested in learning much more.

My limited experience also applies to conversations with girls. "Is that Katherine with a *K* or *C*?"

Nice lead-in!

"Does it really matter?" she says with a giggle and then grabs my hand and pulls me into one of the front rooms where another bar runs along the wall. "Hey, get my new friend a beer, would you?" she shouts over the thumping music to the guy behind the bar, who looks me over and then shrugs and pours me a sloppy draft of whatever keg hides behind the bar.

We chat away. Or mostly, she chats, and I listen, which is okay since I'm nervous and also distracted by her display and trying super-duper hard not to look down. As the minutes tick by, it comes out that she dated Adam for a while earlier in the semester, but he'd been a bit too handsy a few times and not particularly nice to her on other occasions, so she broke it off. That sets off a tiny alarm bell, but I'm still really hoping this is going to go somewhere favorable for me until a few more minutes pass, and it dawns on me that she's more interested in Adam's failure against me in pool than she is in me.

She gives me my out when she leans in close to me again, and I hear her burp as she does so. "Whoops, I just threw up in my mouth a little bit. I might have had a little bit too much to drink. Want to go get another beer? Or maybe find somewhere quiet and make out?" She purrs and nuzzles my ear with soft lips that, sadly, now smell like barf.

"Yeah, you know what? How about I walk you to the bathroom? I'll go find my sister and introduce you two. Do you know her? Morgan? Have you seen her?"

"Oh, she's your sister? Yeah, I know Morgan. Everybody does. She's *so* pretty. I saw her, yeah. She was going upstairs with Jimmy a few minutes ago."

That sets the alarm bell off like a submarine Klaxon. Adam's smirk when he backed down from kicking my ass, his walking back through the crowd with Jimmy, Adam being handsy with Katherine-with-a-*K*-or-*C*.

I tell her I have to go. "Which way is to the stairs?"

She points, and I immediately force my way through the pulsing crowd of kids, still seeking my sister and hoping there's nothing to be worried about, and she can take care of herself. The sinking feeling in my stomach tells me to hurry, and I get less polite as I go and find the stairs leading to the second floor. Students are lined up on the steps, talking, kissing, or talking about kissing, and I have to weave through all of them until I get to the quieter hallway at the top. This is a large house to hold a fraternity, especially a big one like this for the football team, and there are doors running away from me on both sides of the hallway, most of them open, and then the hallway turns ninety degrees and keeps going. I hustle down, peering into rooms as I go, seeing nothing, and stop at a closed door on the left. The couple of beers haven't exactly sharpened me, and I simply turn the knob and walk in without thinking about why it's closed. Whoops! I'm greeted with the sight of a naked couple in mid-coitus, the girl straddling the boy with her arms stretched high above her head. I stand there stupidly, staring at actual fully-naked-this-time boobs for a few seconds until the guy notices me and shouts at me to get out.

Resuming my search, I keep going down the hall, pass the elbow of the turn, and am now beyond the pervasive sound of the music from downstairs. All the doors are open except for the last one at the end of a ratty red runner. This time, I listen before acting, leaning my head up close to the six-paneled door and picking up the strands of conversation from within.

" … think you're so fucking smart, bringing that dipshit kid in here to embarrass me and take our money. Nobody comes into our house and makes us look bad. Nobody! I'm going to teach you a lesson right here, and then the rest of the boys are too. Hold her still! Jeez, can't the four of you handle one girl?"

It sounds like Adam, though it's hard to tell for sure. But, no matter who it is, what I just heard means someone is in trouble, and I'm going in there. By now, I'm sure this is where Morgan is, and this does not sound good. I'm scared and mad and scared. There are five guys in there, and all of them are going to be bigger than me.

All good-quality pool cues are made up of two pieces that screw together rather than the generic one-piece starter cues. Movies show people fighting in bars with cues, snapping them off against the bad guy, but it's misleading. If you hold the skinny end and swing, you'll barely have a grip, and if you hold the fat end, you'll be hitting someone with a stick not much wider than a finger. But using the fat bottom end only of a two piece, that's something to be reckoned with. I slide my case open quickly and quietly, remove the lower half, and grip it hard in my now-sweating right hand, with the thinner end in my grasp. Like most doors, this one opens in, and I cautiously grasp the knob and give it a test turn.

Nothing. Locked.

There are no other options; it's time for my own movie moment. I move back a few steps, deciding whether to try and kick the door near the knob, but that's an awkward angle, so I just rush the door as fast as I can and lead with my left shoulder at impact.

Everything happens faster than it takes to tell the story.

The door explodes in, the pieces of the frame by the knob shattering into fragments as it all lets loose under the force of 170 pounds of desperate kid. Luckily, I don't fall down but stumble to a stop just inside the threshold and am met by the sight of four stunned college football players holding my undressed sister down on a bed against the far wall, and Adam's naked backside in front of me. He must have been walking toward the bed, and it's more than obvious what's going to happen, so I don't hesitate. Before he can turn around, I bring the pool cue down with everything I have against his right kidney area, and he falls to the ground with a howl. For a split second, I think about hitting him on the back of the head, but maybe killing someone isn't a good plan. I need this to stop, and fast, get my sister out of there, and not have police show up to arrest me for murder.

Jimmy's next, holding one of Morgan's legs down on the left side of the bed, and before he can get up, I strike again, bringing the club down on his nearest forearm with a vicious blow, and hear a dull *snap*. He clutches his now-broken arm to his torso and cries out, releasing Morgan. The other three are so shocked by what's happening, they let go and stand up fast, indecisive now that things are going much differently than they planned, with the violence directed toward them instead. I'm a little unsure myself since, even though I've taken Jimmy out of the fight for sure, there's about a thousand pounds of football player in the room with us, and this can still turn out very badly.

"*Who the fuck wants to be next?*" I scream as loud as I can, my voice breaking into a screech at the end. I'm terrified, my veins are coursing with adrenaline, and my heart's racing faster than I've ever felt it. I swing the pool cue wildly at the kid on the same side of the bed as Jimmy and miss, but he scrambles away over the corner of the bed and runs out the door. The two on the far side of the bed pause for a second and then decide leaving is smarter than staying, so they follow right after him. Morgan's scrambling to cover herself with the sheet, and I can hear her sobbing with fear and relief.

Brandishing the cue above my head, I swing back to Adam and Jimmy. Jimmy is out of it, rocking back and forth on the ground, holding his arm with tears streaming down his face. I find out later that he's the team's star quarterback and actually has pro prospects I've likely just ended. Adam stares at me, holding one hand against his back, and without saying a word, he clearly realizes that getting into a fight when naked is a losing proposition. So he covers himself with the other hand and moves off to a corner of the room.

While keeping a side-eye on him in case he changes his mind, I turn back to Morgan. She's wound the sheet around her to cover up and clutches her clothes in a rumpled pile against her body, weeping as she stumbles out the door. I let her go, and she ducks into the first open room, closes the door, and emerges a minute or two later fully dressed yet disheveled.

I've picked up the other half of my pool cue in the meantime, slipping it back into the case and still watching the door of the other room as the adrenaline begins to wane. There's a part of me that wants to go back in there and kill them—teenage logic is pretty black and white, and I'm so angry, I'm not thinking clearly. I've never seen my sister in danger and frightened before, and it has frightened me, too, that they'd do something like that over something as stupid as money and a game of pool. Over my next decade or so, and especially after the mess of the world the zombies make, I learn that the human capacity for being shitty to his fellow human being is boundless, but at this time, I'm appalled by them.

Tonight, we walk out with arms wrapped around one another, Morgan leaning heavily against me and shaking as we move back through the maze of college kids having fun, none of them with an inkling of what just went on a few feet above their heads. We finally get outside, breathing in the clear, crisp, fall air and start walking back to her dorm.

"Morgan," I start to ask, "did they ...?"

She shakes her head softly but doesn't turn to face me and speaks in a low, shaking voice. "No, you got there just in time. I was so scared. Trapped. I've never been helpless before. They could do whatever they wanted to do to me, but I think it was the being confined part that made it even worse."

I want to go back and burn their house down ... maybe with them inside it. We keep walking, though, and get back to her room. Both of us get ready for bed, me sleeping on the floor, and she flicks the lights off. I'm not going to sleep any time soon and instead lie on my back, watching the ceiling and listening to Morgan breathe.

A few minutes after I think she's gone to sleep, she quietly says, "Hey ... thank you."

We've never mentioned that night again, until now. "That time" is why Morgan used to go to women's support groups and tried to anonymously help those women. Why there's a simmering anger in my sister when someone is being taken advantage of or mistreated. Why we're going back to the fortress and doing what we can, no matter how crappy the odds are, to help those people because some of them, especially the women, are trapped, too, and somebody needs to do something to help them.

It's probably not going to go well, ideas like this never do, but we're going. To a walled compound full of men with guns and bad intent. A wonderful idea that I'm sure is going to turn out to be a walk in the park.

CHAPTER 6

Packing doesn't take much time; we're good at it by now. All six of us can fit into the big, black Ford truck with as much gear as we want to haul with us. Weapons, lots of weapons, and ammunition, food for at least ten days, water, flashlights, dark clothing, rope, and extra gas cans. Basically, if it has a potential use, we toss it into the bed of the pickup.

After a day of prep work, we lock all the cabins and hit the road, heading south and west. It'll take us two solid days to make the drive of about twelve hundred miles. Morgan has told us a good bit about the place, so we know the basic structure—a square of houses that has been cleverly joined by cinder-block walls two stories high to form a fortress of sorts—the population (about twenty), and that about half of those people don't seem to want to be there except for the safety-from-zombies factor. I'm not sure how she plans on getting about ten more people into the truck, but she reminds me that all cars are free these days if we can find one with a fresh battery and gas.

We plan as we drive since we have plenty of time. There's no way Morgan can go in since she pissed off the leader, Marcus, when she'd stopped by on her way to New York and made him look bad in front of his followers. I could go but won't be interesting to him. Useful maybe if I have time to become an insider as one of his guards, but we don't plan on dragging this out if we don't have to. It probably makes the most sense to send me in, and then I'll find a way to get people out somehow.

"I should go in," volunteers Eve from the back seat. "Me and Amy can go. They'll never suspect the two of us, and if we go in together, they probably won't separate us at first while we get acclimated." She looks at me. "Every move you made would be watched, and they'd be suspicious about why someone on his own for a couple of years would decide to join a group. He'd see you as a threat."

She's right. But to send the two least physical people in? To a fortress that has one door blocked by a bus, and the other likely heavily guarded as well? There's an opening in the wall that's about six feet wide where they park a bus in front of and move when needed. One of the women Morgan had met told her about a door on the opposite side for emergencies. All sixteen houses that make up the compound face outward, and all their doors and windows have been secured, save one that's locked and dead bolted but not barricaded. That's probably going to be how we get people out, though it means whoever's on the inside will have to overpower at least one guard, and quietly. The idea makes me skeptical and nervous, and I say so.

"But don't you understand?" Eve argues. "A woman and a younger child traveling together, stumbling upon their place, humble and thankful for the shelter and safety. They'll never even entertain the notion that we're up to something other than 'save us' if what Morgan says about the leader is true. We'll be left alone for a few days too. There's no way he'll try anything at first. I bet he wants people to get used to being safe from the outside, and whatever they're running from, and therefore, deeply thankful. Then when he comes to take tribute, they're deciding between something that will be over in a few minutes or being cast outside again."

Unfortunately, from my leadership perspective—I feel it's my job to watch everyone and ensure their safety—this is all making a lot of sense.

Morgan has explained the "tribute," too, after having it explained to her in a brief conversation with one of the residents. This had happened when they'd broken away from the group to go to the restrooms. Once a month, every female has to have sex with Marcus or one of his two key guards; one of those seems unwilling to exact it, but the other is a rough thug who mixes additional pain into the sessions. The idea of it sickens me, and I fight away images of Eve being assaulted and very reluctantly agree to the plan. It's quiet in the truck for a good while afterward as we each ramble down whatever nervous paths our brains are taking us to.

***

The summer day drifts by outside, and we make good progress as the country flattens out. We've found over the years that the highways in general aren't the clogged collections of metal, glass, and rubber you see in post-apocalypse movies. Sure, in some places, we have to leave the road for the shoulder to get around something, but people in cars at highway speeds don't get attacked by zombies. People on foot do, so we're able to keep to a fairly steady fifty miles an hour and just watch for obstructions ahead.

We pass the first day without incident, stopping only for bathroom and food breaks and to pump gas out from the underground tanks at service stations. We can go around four hundred miles on a tank, fully loaded as we are, and we make a note to fill up when we hit the city so we can run for several hours if we have to bug out in a hurry.

By the end of the first day, we've covered nearly seven hundred miles and pull into a rest stop as daylight turns to dusk, scout it out, and park right in the middle of the enormous and empty 18-wheeler section of the lot to take advantage of sight lines in all directions and the bright full moon peeking over the horizon. Sleeping arrangements aren't great in a truck, but we convince the dogs to hop out and get up into the bed with me for the first watch so the women inside will be more comfortable. They bracket me, lying down and resting their muzzles on their front paws, but I see their ears rotating and twitching as they keep alert to the sounds in the night. I rest against the cab of the truck, rifle across my legs, pistol at my side, KNIFE—complete with Australian accent; just can't seem to call it a regular "knife," thank you, Crocodile Dundee—in its holster on my right leg, shotgun against my other leg, ready to make a shitload of noise if needed. The girls settle down quickly, and I sit quietly as night creeps along, a dark specter of watchfulness, scanning all directions to make sure nothing threatens my people. I think about our plan, and it seems a good one, though there's always the unknown we'll probably have to deal with, but we'll contend with that when it happens.

***

The morning erupts to life over the eastern horizon, waking us all up bright and early. Morgan relieved me in the wee hours to keep watch, and she peers in through the back window of the truck and smiles as she sees us stir. We eat a quick, boring, after-zombie breakfast, do the necessaries off in the bushes at the edges of the rest area, and hit the road again. We have five hundred miles or so to go today, and we're anxious to arrive in daylight since headlights will be a dead giveaway from miles away nowadays, given that all the world goes dark when the sun takes a break.

The drive is uneventful. We drive with the windows down to enjoy the day and pass a few abandoned cars and trucks on the way. There are no zombies so far, just an ordinary little road trip to go pick a fight. Planning continues as we get closer, and when we see the first sign with "SAFETY→" spray-painted on an exit sign, we reverse course, drive back to the prior exit, and leave the highway. As usual, there are a few gas stations right at the foot of the ramp, and we swing in to refill the truck for the second time of the day and grab some more water from the no-longer refrigerated cases. Our plan is to drive within half a mile to the fortress, find a good house for Morgan, the dogs, and me to have as our base, and then Amy and Eve will walk the rest of the way.

Luckily, we've thought to bring backpacks to complete their "disguise" of wanderers who're making their way across the country to Colorado for the protection and space in the rough terrain and cold the state will provide, but whose car has broken down a day before. The rest of their backstory is fine mostly as is: survivors from North Carolina and Pennsylvania who've been hiding but decided to cross to the cold weather during the summer to have time for the trip and find a good safe place out west. Sometimes, it's best to just leave out some of the details rather than fabricate a complicated lie that requires remembering.

We leave the station, driving as slowly as we can through the streets of suburbia, scouting each intersection to make sure we don't get spotted by a patrol, and finally get to an area Morgan recognizes. "This is close enough. Let's stop here. It should be about a ten-to-fifteen-minute walk."

I back the truck into the driveway of a blue two-story home, and after clearing the house to confirm there are no critters lurking, I pull the garage-door release and roll the truck inside. Now we're totally out of sight. It's still early in the afternoon, so Eve and Amy pack their backpacks and rub a little dirt on their faces and hands, and all of us leave to follow Morgan.

Once we get roughly halfway, we let them go ahead on their own and branch off onto a parallel street to trail behind, but keeping them loosely in view between abandoned houses. Morgan shushes me and the dogs to silence and creeps to the edge of a house. We peer around it, and I get my first look. It's everything she described—several houses across, cinder-block walls filling the gaps and rising to the height of the rooflines, with the small gap in the middle that's blocked by the side of a city bus with steel plates welded to the bottom so nothing can crawl beneath, and bars affixed to the windows. "SAFETY" is spray-painted high on the wall to the left of the bus in wavering black letters, and there's no one outside.

On the wall on the other side of the doorway is a dark form about five feet off the ground, but from this distance, we can't clearly make out what it is. From here, we can see Eve and Amy walking toward the entrance, shielding their eyes from the sun, moving steadily and holding hands. I'm sure they're as nervous as I am, and I realize I'm holding my breath. They reach the "door" and stop, looking around uncertainly. Nothing happens.

Is it empty? Has this trip been for nothing?

Suddenly, a shrill whistle sounds from behind the walls, and we hear the rattle-rumble of the big bus's diesel engine being started. Eve and Amy stand still, tiny figures in the distance, and I fight the urge to shout for them to forget it and come back so we can get out of here. God, this is a terrible idea.

Morgan senses my unease and grabs my arm firmly before I leave our cover. "We have to. Those people are trapped. He tells them they're safe but *rapes* them," she whispers.

She's right, I know this, but it doesn't make me feel any better. I watch as the bus slides to the side and a gaggle of people emerge from behind the safety of the walls. Two big men with rifles flow out to flank them, scanning the surrounding area for danger and paying little attention to the new arrivals. Assorted other shapes meander outside, and then they part in the middle to allow a single man clear passage.

Marcus.

Tall, blond, moving with ease—it can't be anyone else. We can't hear anything from where we are, the wind has shifted so it's behind us, but we see him throw his hands out to the side in obvious welcome, waving toward his followers and the building. After a few minutes, all of them go back inside with Marcus leading and Eve and Amy to his side, and the crowd closes back up to get through the entrance, and we lose sight of our companions. With a few more glances at the perimeter, the two armed men walk backward and inside. The bus moves back into place, and everything goes fully quiet again.

Morgan and I creep backward out of direct sight, and find an empty house with windows on the back that affords us a view of the front of the fortress, to camp out. It has a second-story deck with a door into the master bedroom, and another ground-level door that empties into the fenced backyard. We draw the blinds closed everywhere except for one window and push a couch to a window in a secondary bedroom with the best line of sight, so we can keep watch as much as we can. The truck with most of our supplies will stay where it is. We'll go back in the dark and collect what we need for weapons and food and use this place as our forward base from which to scout and watch. I'm unsettled and pace the house, unhappy with having Eve and Amy out of sight and being unable to protect them against whatever happens inside the lunatic building. Our friends are inside. Trapped inside a place with "SAFETY" sprayed on the walls but full of dark shadows, lies, and sadness.

Part II

Part II

CHAPTER 7

ve and Amy walk toward the looming structure, holding hands the whole time. As they get close to the outside walls, Amy's hand tightens, and Eve looks to see what has gotten her attention. On the right-hand side of the bus is a body hung on the wall of one of the houses, splayed in crucifixion, several feet off the ground. It's a man in a brown jacket over a white T-shirt and well-worn blue jeans. His hair hangs over his face in dreadlocks tied at the ends with bits of paper, ribbon, and tinsel. On the ground beneath his feet is a pirate hat, of all things, and with a shock, Eve realizes this must be the Jack-the-pirate whom Morgan met on her trip between Colorado and here. He'd escaped and had been walking west when Morgan bumped into him on the highway. He told her about this place and warned her not to stop here. Clearly, they must've tracked him down somehow after Morgan's visit, brought him back here, killed him, and hung him on the wall as an example.

"I'm scared," whispers Amy.

Eve squeezes back in what she hopes is a comforting way but feels deeply uneasy about the dead man hanging in front

of them, a silent warning. "I'm nervous, too, but we're going to be okay. They're going to get us out, and we're going to save some of these people. The people who wouldn't do that to another person. It's going to be two nights and not even a whole second night. Nothing bad can happen in such a short period of time."

The bus moves to the side, and a crowd spills forth and then splits to allow a single man to walk through. He looks carefully at them as he strides forward, a broad, genuine-looking smile on his face, taking powerful strides and then stopping in front of them. "Welcome!" he says in greeting, arms flung wide. Morgan was right, he's handsome and instantly compelling. Well over six feet tall, with an athlete's build and fluidity of movement. Strong cheekbones and bright blue eyes set in a tanned face framed by dirty-blond hair that drapes down to his shoulders. "All are welcome and can find sanctuary and safety here! I'm Marcus, and these are my friends."

He catches Eve's eyes flicking up to the bedraggled corpse on the wall, and his smile falters for a moment and then brightens again. "Ah, our scarecrow. The consequences of betrayal of our safety. I'm sorry you, and the child, are seeing that. We have few, but strict, rules here that are solely for the security of all of us, and that man violated those. Sadly, he had to be made an example so that others will remember their obligation to the group. These days require different measures than those of the past. Please, come inside and rest. You must be tired from your journey, and there is no reason to linger over this … unpleasantness."

Eve nods assent, though her eyes are drawn to the body several times as they all walk forward and through the opening in the wall, and the bus returns to its position as a barrier. It feels like the light of the day dims a bit as they're enclosed, and her heart rate speeds up another tick, and she closes her hand on Amy's even more snugly.

Marcus looks at them warmly. "What are your names?"

"I'm Eve, and this is Amy."

"How pretty. Those are two of my favorite names. I'm glad you found us." He looms over her, not in a threatening way but just with the presence of someone much larger than her. "Where are you coming from?"

"We're from the East. I'm from Pennsylvania but was living in North Carolina when everything happened. I left there to see if I could find my parents back home, and when I got there, I met Amy. We joined up but decided a little while ago that we might be safer out west where it's colder and less populated, so we started driving. Our car broke down though. Maybe bad gas or something, I don't know. We've been walking since yesterday and saw your signs."

"Wonderful," he replies. "I'm happy that they steered you in the right direction. We can keep you safe here and are always pleased to have new members of our tribe. It's good that you reached us before nightfall too. We're still threatened by the monsters fairly often, but you'll be fine inside with us."

He chats more as they walk, telling her about the walls (his idea), the bus (he armored himself), where the bathrooms are, and how many people are there (nineteen), and invites them for dinner. The sun is drooping toward the horizon, and shadows lengthen on the inside of the enormous enclosure, and Eve agrees that a meal would be nice when he offers. They make their way over to a clutch of picnic tables arrayed beneath a sprawling oak tree for shade, and the rest of the group trailing behind them either sit or busy themselves with putting food on the table.

A pale-skinned woman with pin-straight dark hair that reaches her waist is the server for their table, and her oval face is mostly obscured as she sets down plates of freshly grilled vegetables and pours water for all. Eve guesses this must be the woman Morgan described, the one who had told her the truth about Marcus and confirmed what really happens here, and makes a mental note to try and talk to her alone whenever she gets the chance.

Amy is sitting as close to her as possible without being in her lap, and she senses her nervousness and pats her leg reassuringly under the table. Marcus continues talking, regaling her with the good they've done here to provide safety for a group, talking about their rules for staying in groups when venturing outdoors, the occasional attacks by the zombies, though those are largely impotent and uninteresting ones. According to him, they just shuffle around the perimeter of the fort, moaning and scratching at the walls until they lose interest and meander away. He asks questions from time to time, mostly about where they came from, how they survived, and whether there are any other people alive between Pennsylvania and Kansas.

Surreptitiously observing the crowd as she converses with him, Eve notices that almost everyone is eating in silence, speaking only to ask a tablemate to pass something over, but otherwise, their collective heads are down. The pair of big men who had flanked the two of them when they arrived are still on guard of sorts, standing on either side of the dining area with rifles across their chests and watchful eyes. She wonders if those are Marcus's only real allies, the two who participate in the paying of tribute each month—one not doing anything, but the other taking pleasure in it and hurting the women with pinches and rough grabs on top of the sexual humiliation. If so, the odds aren't too bad except they're big, serious, and well-armed.

The plan is fairly simple: do nothing the first night since it's virtually certain they'll be watched and perhaps guarded. The next day, Eve will look for the back door, the door in the one house not barred and barricaded, so they can all escape if needed, and if presented with the opportunity, she must enlist others. That night, she'll find a way to unlock the door to allow the siblings in, and then she'll gather who she can for a midnight escape.

During the drive from New York, they all agreed to this, feeling that staying too long increases the danger of something unpleasant happening as well as a slipup in their story. In and out as quickly as possible and with whoever's willing to leave. Morgan thought they need to make the females a priority, but any men are welcome too.

Marcus leaves their table and circulates among the others, talking animatedly to each table and laying out instructions for tomorrow's chores, defining who's on watch at each of the four corners of the enclosure starting at nightfall. He's working the crowd like an evangelist with smiles and pats on the shoulder. There are seven women sprinkled around the group, all of them younger than about forty, and she notices none of them make eye contact with Marcus as he visits. The dozen men are also on the younger side; the two guards and then ten more regular men. About half of them look directly at their leader as he speaks, and the others keep their eyes on their plates. So that makes about a dozen who aren't happy here, though there's no way to tell the degree of unhappiness. They aren't all going to fit in the truck, that's something to consider, but it encourages Eve, knowing the majority are going to potentially be on her side. Get out first, then figure out transportation and any other details on the fly afterward.

***

Dinner winds down quickly as night begins falling in earnest. Low-light solar landscaping lanterns emerge in unison around their perimeter to help illuminate the clearing of the tables, and a few people carry bright flashlights.

Everyone is beginning to stand up and drift away to the houses on the perimeter for guard duty or bedtime when Marcus makes his way back to them and smiles. "Eve, Amy, please accept our hospitality for the evening. We have a vacant house that is being made up for you as we speak. You'll have it to yourself so that you can be comfortable. Tomorrow, we can talk about long-range plans, but I hope you strongly consider remaining here with us in safety. We can keep you secure here and would love to have you." He looks at one of the guards. "Vince, why don't you take our new arrivals to their quarters and get them settled?"

If Eve didn't know the truth of the situation, she'd feel as welcome as can be. Marcus appears to be nothing of a monster, just charismatic and unthreatening, and she can see how anyone would comfortably decide to stay here behind the tall walls, in a group with a strong leader. It's unsettling to know there's a darker side to all of this, and she's glad they've come to rescue some of these people from their safe trap. She smiles in return and thanks him politely, and they follow Vince to a house on the rear wall. She's pleased by this since it'll be near whichever one isn't completely closed to the outside, but she knows that they won't put her in that one since it's probably guarded at night.

Their escort is a football-player-sized man with broad, lumpy, muscular shoulders underneath an impossibly snug T-shirt that strains against his massive arms. He glances over his shoulder once to make sure they're behind him and then stops at the doorway to a house that's one removed from the corner of the enclosure.

After opening the door, he steps back to let them enter and hands Eve a small flashlight and canteen of what she assumes is water, but then he follows them indoors. Resting his rifle against the doorframe and pulling out a pistol and flashlight of his own, he motions for them to wait and sweeps the house efficiently before returning to the foyer. "The bedrooms are upstairs. I'd suggest taking the one to the left of the landing since it's on an inside wall. Those fucking zombies come around every once in a while and moan their stupid shit outside, so it's a little quieter on the inside rooms if they come for a visit."

He has a gravelly voice that escapes through a dense beard covering most of his face. Brown eyes beneath a baseball hat pulled low watch her steadily and, she notices unhappily, with hunger. "Before you go up," he continues, "I'm gonna search you. We check everyone for weapons. Not that they're not allowed, but we're makin' sure we know what we got for guests. Stand still, right there. Turn around," he says to her as he holds the compact flashlight in his teeth and the pistol in one hand so the threat is subtle but clear.

Eve would normally have told him to piss off, but she knows she has to quietly go along and holds her tongue. Their plan depends on them being seen as an innocuous pair of females in distress, stranded by their car, seeking safety, and thankful for the rescue. She turns around and subconsciously closes her eyes. A big hand makes its way up and down her sides, sweeps around to the front of her torso, and grabs her breasts in turn with a brief, sharp pinch at each of her nipples.

So he's obviously the grabbing one.

She holds still as he moves around to face her, her eyes open now and making unflinching contact with his. He doesn't seem to notice or care and continues to pat her down to the ankles. As he stands back up, he reaches between her legs and cups her roughly there for a few seconds, fingers wiggling as he stares down at her. "Gotta make sure there's nothing right there that shouldn't be." He smirks as his fingers keep pushing upward against her and then he finally stops.

Eve breathes a sigh of relief, but then for a terrifying moment, she fears he'll subject Amy to the same invasive search. While she's young, she's beginning to bud into young womanhood. Thankfully, he completely ignores her. Vince quickly paws through her backpack, finds nothing of interest, and tosses it indifferently to the floor. He packs up his gear, steps to the door of the house, and then looks back over his shoulder at Eve. "It's going to be a pleasure gettin' to know *you* better."

CHAPTER 8

Morgan and I watch our friends disappear inside, followed by the bus moving back into place. The walls of the enclosure are just as tall as all the other buildings in the area, so we have no way of seeing what's going on inside but hope introductions are as pleasant, largely, as they were when Morgan had stopped before. Settling back from the window since there's nothing to do now but wait, we decide that when it gets fully dark, we'll go collect our additional weapons and food from the truck and then alternate naps over the next hours to get rested up for what's going to be a long, careful night. We'll be doing the same thing tomorrow, too, since there won't be anything for us to do during the day.

I rest first until nightfall, and then we creep out of our forward post and make it to where we've stored the truck without any problem. I decide to leave the keys in the ignition so if, for any reason, we're separated before we leave, whoever gets here will at least have an escape vehicle. We make sure the house is secure, and leave one door unlocked but with a piece of firewood resting against the base to clue us in if anyone was there while we're away.

As we move back toward the other house, I hear Ajax give a little grumble deep in his throat, like a dog whisper, and I freeze on the spot and reach an arm over to Morgan as well. We're heavily loaded with all our gear, which is going to be a liability in a fight, so I step from the concrete of the sidewalk onto the adjacent lawn and kneel down. Slowly, very slowly, placing my duffle bags filled with guns, water, and snacks on the soft grass, I pull my .45 from the waistband of my jeans and KNIFE from its sheath, doing all I can to move as stealthily as possible and stay in a crouched position. Morgan does the same, and the dogs step closely to our sides so we're all facing in a different direction. There's little breeze and virtually no moonlight yet, but I reach out with my senses to "see" what's out there to cause alarm for the dog. It takes a minute, but I finally pick up the faint scent of decay that always comes with one of the walking corpses plaguing the planet, and a moment later, I hear their distinctive shuffling steps scuffing asphalt. One, two, maybe three of them are out there but not too close, and we're downwind of them, so they'll never pick up our scent. I lean in close to Morgan and ask if she hears them too. She nods and gestures toward our forward house. Any kind of a fight out here will be noisy, and sound carries well now that the constant background noise of the world has been silenced.

After a handful of silent minutes, we reclaim our gear and move on, staying in the middle of the streets to avoid stumbling over any lawn debris or landscaping decorations in the dark. We finally make it back to our new place, locking the door behind us and exhaling with relief. "That was fun," Morgan says with a grin.

"If you say so," I reply. Morgan's idea of fun has always been a bit different than everyone else's. She's like a stuntwoman being filmed 24/7. "Let's get set and go scout them out. See what they have for light, if any, how many sentries they have posted, and finish by working out our route from their back door to the truck." We need to be ready to move in a hurry when we leave, and if we collect some new people, groups never move expeditiously, so a direct flight would be best. I hope we won't be fighting our whole way there, or at all.

Dropping most of our gear in the upstairs bedroom, we blacken our faces and hands with some soot from the cold fireplace and then tell the dogs to stay. We'll do the same the next night so we take no chance of one of them seeing a squirrel or something and making an unwelcome racket. Neither of them like that idea and whine as we're closing the door, but we need a practice run on all counts. We move like wraiths in the night and start to circle from a two-block distance, keeping to the shadows as much as possible. The moon looms large and bright tonight behind intermittent cotton-ball clouds, with the faint breeze still pushing in from the west. Increasing humidity lurks densely over the evening, forewarning of a likely weather change for tomorrow. I hadn't planned for that—not like we could check our phones for the forecast anymore. Like many things nowadays, you go with what's delivered and work it out from there.

We took one final step indoors to make sure anything that will jingle or rattle is secured as well. The truck keys are out of my pocket and back in the truck, spare clips for my .45 are in separate pockets, and even our shoelaces are tucked inside our shoes. We don't want to make noise of any kind and alert the home team they have guests beyond Amy and Eve.

Morgan and I did stuff like this way back when we were kids. The road we'd grown up on was a winding one about two miles long that eventually petered out into the woods, with houses on one side and undeveloped land on the other that stretched for miles. At the time, the small towns that surrounded the larger New York City suburbs were lightly populated, and there were only a few neighbors. Most of those were people from the city who had second homes on this upstate lake and rarely visited. There were a couple of other kids who lived nearby, and the two of us would stay up late, wait for them to walk by in a small group in the night, and then sneak slowly up on them from behind to scare the shit out of them. We thought it was funny, anyway, playing ninja.

The stakes are higher now. Any screams are going to count this time, so we skulk in the shadows of the looming suburban trees and check each side of the walls, noting that there's no light coming from inside, which makes sense. The world is so dark now with the absence of artificial light that any nighttime illumination stands out like a floodlight; we do the same thing and stay dark after sundown as much as we can so we don't attract the boogey monsters. I notice a couple of heads silhouetted atop the walls in the light of the ascending moon, one on each of the first three sides. It takes us close to fifteen minutes per side to move as quietly as we need to while keeping sight of the guards. As we're about to get around to the front of the hodgepodge of a building, we have to cross the road leading toward the front "door," which is now well lit by the moon, which means we'll be exposed for a moment or two, and so we sink to a crouch and hold a whispered conversation.

"We should go farther away into those streets, a couple of blocks in, and then cross," I say.

"I'm bored from sneaking around and ready to go back and get some rest," she answers. "Let's just run across quickly, together rather than one at a time. They'll have trouble noticing unless they just happen to look at the right time. We're fast."

I'm watching the walls as she speaks and notice that, in contrast to the other sides, there are three heads along this stretch of the enclosure; two on our side of the entrance and one on the farther side. A good sign for tomorrow since they're clearly more focused on the front door than the back. Bad odds for right now, but I have an idea. "Nope. Let's hide in plain sight. We saw those zombies earlier, or heard them anyway. They're going to be used to having them wandering around. Let's play zombie and just walk right across the road under their noses. Let's see what happens, but be ready to haul ass just in case they decide it's time for target practice."

And so tonight, we play zombie, stuttering out into the street and mimicking their meandering walk, holding our weapons close to our bodies as we slowly cross toward the far sidewalk and dense shadows again. Not a peep from the fortress behind us, though about halfway across, I hear Morgan stifle a snicker. Then she stops with a suppressed gasp, turns toward the front wall. A shadowy figure hangs there. From our lookout, we weren't able to see it clearly, but now, even in the moonlight, we can see it's a person crucified on the wall.

"Jack ..." she whispers. I push her in the back. We can't stop here; we're entirely exposed. "That bastard!" Less of a whisper this time, so I push her harder toward the far side of the street, listening for any sort of alarm from the walls. She finally moves forward, though casts more than one glance over her shoulder.

Once we cross safely, we head back to our new house, moving a little more quickly than we were before since we're now out of earshot of the guards, when I bump into the back of my sister. I freeze, knowing she's heard or seen something, and once again slowly draw my pistol out from where it's tucked into the back of my jeans, feeling the seep of adrenaline in my muscles.

We stand stock-still for a minute, then two, and then we see a group of zombies, maybe ten of them walk right down the middle of the street toward the front wall, mill around there aimlessly for a bit, and then wander off into the darkness around the corner.

We wait again, ears straining against the silence, until we're satisfied and go the rest of the way home. I ask her who that crucified person is, and she explains it's Jack-the-pirate.

He must have been caught somehow, even though she'd met him more than one hundred miles from here. She's furious, stomping around the house and describing everything she's going to do to Marcus when she gets the chance. I let her steam and then cool down since that's usually the way to handle things with her. The dogs are pleased to see us, and we let them out for a quick pee, and then we slowly settle in for the evening, alternating watches and sleep since we have a lot of time to kill.

***

A thunderclap rudely wakes me the next morning, and I open my eyes to a sullen day. A slate-gray sky sprawls out as far as I can see, with heavier dark clouds pregnant with moisture looming on the western horizon. Rain starts just a minute later, and not just any rain. It's like a mammoth bucket has been upended over our house all at once, or as our grandfather liked to say, to the chagrin of our mother, "It was pouring like a cow pissing on a rock." This won't be helpful if it keeps up all day, though now that I think about it, it may provide additional cover that night from the moon's gaze and for any sound, so maybe it's a good thing.

I slip my running shoes on—I'd slept fully clothed except for those because, you know, zombies—and leave my room to find Morgan. I come across her in the family room on the ground floor, curled up in a bright-purple blanket in front of a large bay window and reading a romance novel, of all things. An impossibly heroic, shirtless man with flowing locks, and who looks suspiciously like Fabio, stands commandingly above a red-haired damsel in distress (barely) clad in a magenta-and-white Victorian gown on the cover. Morgan tucks a bookmark with a picture of a lighthouse on it into the middle of the paperback and sets it to the side when I come into the room.

"A romance novel, Morgan?"

"Yes!" she says with a big sleepy smile. "There are tons of them in the house, and this is the newest Lewis one. I haven't read it yet." She's practically bubbling. My badass, überathletic, in-your-face-about-everything, competitive-to-the-point-of-insanity sister is bubbling about having found the most recent *romance novel?* "A girl can hope, you know."

Um, okay. Didn't see that one coming.

CHAPTER 9

The same thunderclap startles Eve up and out from the depths of sleep, but Amy is unmoving, breathing deeply beside her. The night before, Amy was nervous about what they're doing, and the scene with Vince had unnerved her even further, so she sought the comfort of company and snuggled against Eve like when they'd spent the winter in Pennsylvania. If Eve is being honest with herself, she's happy for the girl's close presence since she, too, is frightened. She has unwavering faith in the siblings, but they're outnumbered, there are walls to deal with, and the weather now feels like a harbinger of misfortune.

Since Morgan only spent an hour or so here, Eve has no idea what these people do on a daily basis but supposes it's like what they do—gather food, weapons, and water and keep on the lookout for zombies ... and tribute. She thinks about that as she wishes for coffee to clear the mental cobwebs. Supposedly, once a month, each of the women here—Eve counted seven yesterday—are obligated to have sex, or something, with Marcus or one of his two guards. Vince obviously enjoys being one of the insiders, but one of the women had told Morgan that the other one doesn't participate. The idea revolts Eve; "consensual" rape sounds worse than other forms since the women will know it's coming, and she can only imagine their thoughts on those days.

Now fully shaken from sleep, thanks to these unpleasant thoughts, she slides quietly out of the bed, taking care not to disturb Amy. The windows of the house are open, at least toward the center of the open space inside the walls, and she smells the rain as it pours over the overwhelmed gutters and spatters onto the patio behind the house. She eases the bedroom windows closed to let the child sleep, shrugs on a second shirt over the top of the one she slept in, and leaves the bedroom to see what else may be in the house for food, or hopefully, caffeine.

As if someone is watching her through the window, there's a discreet tap on the French door leading to the patio. She looks out to see Marcus standing under an enormous golf umbrella held in one hand and a thermos in the other. He smiles at her through the glass, a broad, winning grin that lights his handsome face despite the scowling weather that rages behind him.

Moving quickly to unlock and open the door, she steps back to let him inside and to avoid the flinging downpour. He ducks in quickly, putting the umbrella near the door and shrugging out of his windbreaker.

"Good morning," he says quietly. "Is Amy still asleep?"

Eve nods and wonders why he's here. She also wishes she'd gotten fully dressed since she isn't wearing a bra. Even though she has two shirts on, they're thin, and the open door has gusted cool wind inside.

He hands her the thermos and smiles again. "Coffee. Hot and fresh. I thought you might like some, and we've got a clever engineer who's rigged up solar panels to help us with simple things like power for coffee makers. That alone gives him the right to stay here forever! Even though the weather is horrible," he continues with a nod over his shoulder, "they store enough power to be good for about eighteen hours of use if we stick with small things like a coffeepot here."

Out of old habit, and perhaps nerves, Eve goes to the cupboards and finds two coffee mugs and then walks over to the refrigerator and opens it to look for milk.

Marcus chuckles behind her as she sheepishly closes the empty fridge. "I'm afraid we only have so much power, so you can have your coffee any way you like as long as it's black."

His voice is smooth and reassuring with no hint of menace, and Eve wonders how many travelers have come through this settlement over the past years and been comforted and sheltered by this man at first, and then violated at some point later on. She concentrates on keeping her expression impassive as she sips the blessed nectar of morning, mentally thanking the clever engineer since this isn't just instant coffee, but the real thing. If she meets the man, she might give him a hug.

"I hope you slept well here in safety."

She finally speaks up. "Yes, thank you, I did. It was very nice to be able to rest without having to take turns staying up and alert. Just sleep. It was wonderful, like this coffee."

His smile is magnificent. "Oh, Eve. That makes me happy to hear. I'm pleased to be able to provide both coffee and security. And," he adds with a wink, "I'm glad to hear that you are thankful for it." If she didn't know what's behind the wink, she'd have guessed he's lightly flirting with her but nothing more.

They sit in companionable silence on two barstools adjacent to the kitchen island. Happily, the coffee begins to take effect and clears all remnants of rest from Eve's mind. The pantry holds an assortment of granola bars and the like, so she contentedly munches on one of those as well. Anyone who comes here would most likely feel the same way she does right now. Welcomed. Secure, for the first time in ages, behind the walls and guards. Safe. Thankful. And, perhaps most importantly, afraid to go back "out there."

The rain continues its assault outside. These houses have the typical suburban quarter-acre lots, but she can barely see the back end of the yard through the deluge. Eve imagines that rainy days here and now aren't spent any differently than they were before. Stay inside, read, nap, and basically skip the day. But someone will be on guard. They're always on guard against the undead, and she knows she has to be on guard against the living here. It shakes her inside since, in comparison to the lake in New York, where nothing is asked in return for being safe, this is a horrible price to pay.

Marcus suddenly interrupts her thoughts. "Normally, we cover the critical rules with new arrivals as soon as they come. There are some other things about being part of our family, and I usually wait for the right time to go over those, but there has been some unrest here of late. You saw the man hanging on the wall, and while that was unfortunate, it was also a necessary lesson. We ... *I* provide safety here. Food, water, the walls. Coffee," he adds with another gentle smile. "In exchange for those things, everyone is expected to follow simple rules: no one goes outside in a group smaller than five and everyone takes care of their assigned tasks without complaint. We all have daily chores essential to our survival like cleaning, finding food, and so on. We have no other youngsters here like Amy, which hopefully won't prove too boring for her. She will be expected to work like the adults, however. Some members stand guard as their sole responsibility or carry out my directions by proxy, like Vince. All simple enough and understood?"

She nods in agreement.

"There is no delicate way to go over the final rule," he continues, "arguably the most important one. I've tried over time to find different ways to explain it and have decided that the direct route is, well, the most effective. Rip the band-aid off all at once, so to speak. In exchange for food, water, shelter, and the company of a group, there is the matter of rent. I have heard it called 'tribute' by others here but dislike that term since it connotes worship in some manner, and that's inaccurate. Once a month, the residents here are to come to my quarters, bathed and dressed in something ..." he pauses, clearly seeking the right word, "alluring."

He stops again and watches her closely, no doubt waiting for her to understand without being told bluntly. She gives him no such satisfaction and stares back with eyebrows raised in query, but with a racing heart. Eve was sure, the whole group had been sure, that they usually delay this conversation and wait until people get comfortable before forcing them to choose. She hopes he's just going to tell her about it only and not expect anything right now, and works to settle her breathing as much as possible.

He continues after a moment, his eyes flicking down and then up her figure. "Well then. On that night, we will have sex in the method of my choosing. Consensual or otherwise, that choice is yours. The alternative is expulsion since that is the immediate and nonnegotiable penalty for any infractions here. Is that, too, simple enough and understood?"

Eve knows she has to say something, that a new arrival without the benefit of forewarning would protest. "We come here, searching for shelter from those … those monsters out beyond the walls. The ones who *kill* people. There are so few of us left. And you expect that women act as your concubines in return?"

"Well, when you put it in such straightforward terms, yes." Not a hint of guilt or shame on his face. This is his kingdom, and he knows it.

"No goddamn way. This isn't how you treat people. This isn't right. We'll leave as soon as Amy wakes up. Just let us go." She's angry, and it's genuine, so there is no need for her to try and behave as if this is shocking to her. Even with the foreknowledge she had coming in here, this whole arrangement deeply disturbs her, and she glances around surreptitiously for a knife or similar, wishing for a weapon of any kind. This thought, however, surprises her, and she wonders not for the first time what the new world has done to all of them.

He grins, which she doesn't expect. It isn't the gentle, here-I-am-with-morning-coffee-and-conversation   grin either. It's a hungry and triumphant one. "If that is your choice, so be it. But before you make a final decision, you should consider one more facet of the expulsion since you've partaken of our hospitality and are, therefore, subject to our rules. All who leave are stripped bare of their clothes and belongings and left outside the walls to take their chances with a *real* fresh start. This is a lesson for the others. You choose, but you pay the consequences. The world isn't as simple as it was. Consequences are more significant these days. This includes the girl, by the way."

She's shocked, even though she already knew some measure of what he's just said. All of this is delivered in such a conversational tone, it's as if they're still talking about the engineer who had figured out how to power a coffeepot. If she didn't have the siblings outside as small solace, she knows she'd be panicking inside now. As it is, fear slithers insistently into her mind since there's no guarantee their plan will work, and the idea of being trapped here under these conditions is horrifying.

Marcus stands, leaving his coffee mug on the counter. "I'll give you some time to think. Let's say until midday. Then you either stay, and the rent is due tomorrow night, or you leave, and maybe we'll at least give you some sunscreen when you go."

"How? How can you ... force women to have sex with you? All of them here?"

"Eve, you're missing the point. I don't force anyone to have sex. I force them to make a choice. All of them choose to pay the rent. And it's not really about the sex, though that's enjoyable enough, of course. It's about the *submission*. But you might have figured that out for yourself already. Or not. Makes no difference to me. You have about four hours to work it out."

"You're a ... a monster! Worse than the ones outside. At least they don't know what they're doing. They're like animals. You're an animal who plans out what he does!"

"I've been called worse. And *you* get to choose between the monster who is going to have sex with you once in a while, or the ones who are going to kill you and Amy. You see, Eve, you're completely in charge of what happens next. Good luck this morning." He walks toward the front door, and as he reaches it, he swings it open and steps halfway outside while putting his jacket back on and opening his umbrella against the deluge. Before leaving, he stops again and looks back at her. "Oh, and, Eve, one more thing. Everyone pays the rent, but we've never had someone as young as Amy here. So there's one more choice for you. If you stay, you can pick which of you is responsible for paying rent on behalf of *both* of you."

Before she can say another word, he begins to whistle a tune as he turns away and moves back out into the rain, closing the door behind him. Through the window, Eve sees his big form vanish quickly behind the sheets of water pummeling his horrible fortress, and she flings her coffee mug at the door he just closed, shattering the porcelain into hundreds of shards across the room. She can't imagine what life is like for these people here, especially the women, and then she abruptly realizes he had never specifically said *women alone* are obligated to exchange their dignity for safety. A smiling, handsome, charismatic, genial, sanctuary-offering, monstrous being lurks behind these walls, and Eve can't decide if she wants to survive the escape if something goes wrong. She also recognizes what he had been whistling: "Gimme Shelter."

***

Most humans don't really like silence. Eve is generally okay with it and actively seeks solitude each day. In her prior life, her husband traveled for work and was successful enough that she didn't need to have a regular job of her own. Most of her days were spent in their house, though she wasn't a recluse. Exercise at the gym, rounds of golf—with or without partners—and lunches with a small group of close friends mostly filled parts of her days. But she'd otherwise been comfortable indoors as well, no music playing or television left on, and she tended to leave her computer muted as well when she browsed.

This morning, however, the silence looms over her, as if the mammoth-sized, bruised-black thunderheads are hurling their raging downpour inside the house rather than at the earth outside. She paces with the anxious energy of an expectant father. It isn't over the actual decision—she'll say they're staying, of course, since that's what they planned. It's over the endless capacity of people who want to exert and hold power over others and win at the expense of others. Of course, there are many, many good people in the world. Well, not so many now, but it's the assholes you tend to remember in the course of a day, and it seemed like the daily asshole ratio had been growing long before the world had come to a screeching halt. And here's a survivor, someone who could offer something magical for people with his ingenuity to build the compound and provide sustenance for a flock of others, but he chooses to corrupt it. She didn't understand such behavior before; she comprehends it even less under these circumstances.

Her resolve to do whatever needs to be done to get these people out hardens into something she can almost grasp in her angry hands.

*****

We kill time all day long. I clean every gun we have, check the ammunition more times than needed, sharpen the KNIFE, and then sit at the window, watching the building that's scarcely visible as more than a ghostly shadow through the ongoing downpour. Morgan sits downstairs on the couch, polishes off the book, and follows that with a nap for several hours. We planned on alternating watches, and it's her turn, but I let her sleep since I'm too restless to do so myself. The house is indeed full of books, and I had been hopeful until I scanned the shelves to find that all of them are bustier busters. Not to my taste.

I'm worried for Eve and Amy; not that I expect anything bad to happen to them today but rather for what might happen if our simple plan goes awry. We have no idea how many of the residents are loyal to Marcus and, therefore, are possible opponents, so we could be walking (well, sneaking) into a rattlesnake den. I hope enough of them are disgusted at his practices to at least be neutral in a fight, or perhaps, be on our side if it comes to that.

What I really hope is Eve will quietly collect whoever wants to leave during the day, assemble them late at night, and then simply open the back door so we can get out of there without a conflict. She's supposed to initially find the woman who spoke to Morgan when she'd stopped there, and have that woman spread the word of their planned escape. If Eve is seen mingling with a lot of people throughout the first day there, she'll be viewed with suspicion, and the potential escapees may not trust her, so she needs to find the pale woman with dark straight hair. The rain will both complicate and simplify things. It'll limit everyone to being mostly indoors today if it keeps up.

***

Eve and Amy kill time too. Their house has books, a random blend that indicates a family lived here in the past since there's a hodgepodge of young-adult fiction, military thrillers, and popular best sellers to choose from. They decide to whittle away the morning by reading in the weak light allowed through the windows by the relentless storm.

After some time, just as they're feeling hungry and looking in the pantry for something more substantial than granola bars, there's a tap at the door. Eve goes to greet the visitors, mindful that she hasn't cleaned up the debris from the coffee mug from earlier, so she ducks to sweep it up quickly before she opens the door. There's a clutch of people this time. Marcus, his thug Vince, and the woman who was the server at the meal yesterday. She's pretty in a delicate way, with skin even paler than Eve's, straight dark hair, and oval face that suggest a hint of Asian heritage mixed somewhere in her genealogy. She carries a large covered pot in both hands and shuffles past Eve to deposit it on the stove, and then collects bowls from one of the upper cabinets. Once she's done, she stands off to the side, and when she subconsciously brushes her hair away from her face, Eve notices the remnants of a dark bruise encircling her right eye and feels a flame of renewed anger.

Vince takes up a position next to the door, cradling his shotgun in his arms and looking Eve over thoroughly, and then his gaze dances overlong on Amy, telling Eve that Marcus has explained their conversation of the morning. She suspects that while "the rent" is about power for both men, Vince takes more pleasure in humiliation than the actual act. She shudders on the inside and says a silent prayer that they'll all get out of here safely.

Marcus smiles and extends his arms to the side, like he had when welcoming them. "I bring you some soup for lunch on this rainy day! Not from cans but rather what we've grown ourselves in a little garden, plus fresh chicken.

One of our residents was a farmer in the past, and we have a flock of them here for eggs and food. I hope you enjoy it. Let's all sit in the dining room and get further acquainted as well as see what you've decided."

Nothing like getting right to the point.

After the woman scoops hearty portions of the steaming soup into their bowls, the five of them settle at a sprawling table that's nearly too large for the dining room—Marcus at the head, Vince and the woman to his right, Eve and Amy to his left. They tuck into the food, which is utterly delicious and rich; it's the first real meal they've had in literally years. *It might actually be worth it,* Eve thinks in a delirious flicker as the amazing food hits her taste buds, *to have the safety of the walls, the security of a group, and food like this.* It isn't a serious thought, but she can understand how someone might make that choice.

Marcus interrupts her thoughts. "I've neglected my manners. This is Kuniko," he says with a gesture to the still-silent woman. "She is a skilled cook and takes pleasure in serving others."

Vince snorts at this, and Eve glances sideways at Amy to see if she picked up the real meaning of this. The child, thankfully, seems oblivious, eating the soup as if it's her first meal in days, a small dribble of the broth sliding down her chin.

"Kuniko," Marcus continues, "will fill you in on the details that I may not have covered earlier. Some things are better explained to women by women. That is, I assume, if you have come to a decision?"

"I have," Eve says, trying to phrase her answer carefully so Amy won't become even more nervous than she was the night before. She tries to keep an impassive expression on her face as well, though it's a struggle to suppress her scathing anger at him. "We'd be thankful for your hospitality and would like to join your group."

"Wonderful! And the matter of rent?"

"What does that mean? We don't have any money," interjects Amy.

Shit. "He means that we'll have to work, like everyone else here, to earn our keep. I, uh, will have to do some extra work since I'm older."

Vince and Marcus exchange a smirk. Kuniko keeps her head down, busying herself with her food, her hair forming a curtain over her eyes.

Marcus looks back at Eve. "Eve, that pleases me greatly. We'll be happy to have new residents. Kuniko will get you up to speed on your ... work for tomorrow."

Kuniko glances at her out from behind her screening hair, making eye contact but remaining silent.

"We'll leave you now to have that conversation."

With that, Marcus and Vince take a last bite of their soup, stand, and bustle out of the room, Vince taking care to retrieve the shotgun he left at the front door as they go.

Kuniko stands and gathers the abandoned bowls and brings those into the kitchen without a word, though Amy follows her and asks if there's more, which there is. Once she refills Amy's bowl and returns to the dining room, Kuniko tips her head toward the stairs leading to the second floor.

Eve gets up to follow, and they go up to the bedroom, well out of earshot.

"Why did you come here?" Kuniko's voice is soft but urgent. "Why did you agree to stay? Do you understand what he means by 'the rent'?"

"I do. He explained it to me, rather bluntly, this morning," Eve answers. She feels confident this is the woman Morgan met, who risked everything by telling Morgan the truth, and so Eve feels she can trust her with her own truth. "I'm not here to stay. You met a woman in a red Corvette a short while ago. I'm with her and her brother. They're outside the walls, waiting to take us out of here with whoever else you think wants to leave. Tonight. We have to get everyone together and open the back door for them, and then we can take you all somewhere truly safe."

"Morgan? You're with Morgan?" she asks with a hint of a rueful smile. "She made Marcus and Vince really mad when she stopped here. Took Vince's dog and made him look bad for not searching her properly for weapons. Made Marcus angry for not staying and for offering to take some of us with her then. He outsmarted her a bit, saying only one could go and that he'd choose who it was from whoever stepped forward. We all knew that he'd let one go but punish the rest, so no one moved. He was also mad about Jack, both that he'd gotten away and told someone about us here. You can see how that turned out. Poor, crazy, harmless Jack."

"Yes. Morgan insisted we come here to get you out. We have a truck, weapons, and somewhere good to go. Do you think you can get the word out to the right people today, and safely? How many do you think would want to leave?"

"I can tell people. Marcus trusts me. He thinks I've given in, so I have the run of the compound with the responsibility for distributing food," she answers. "I haven't given in, you know. But it's safe here, and there's food, and a few good people. And the other part, it's over after a few minutes unless it's Vince." She breaks eye contact with Eve as she says the last.

"Kuniko, there's nothing to be ashamed of. You haven't done anything wrong. We're here to help, but we need your help too. How many?" Eve reaches out to the other woman and rests a hand against her arm, trying to comfort and encourage her.

Kuniko removes a black hair band from her wrist and sweeps her hair back away from her face into a high ponytail. She's lovely, with faint green eyes that are slightly almond shaped sitting atop high cheekbones. Eve guesses her age to be about thirty, like her, and her own eyes explore the angry bruise on the other woman's face in sympathy.

"I think six or seven others that I can be sure of. There are two women that aren't safe to talk to. The sort that don't seem to mind the arrangement and might even go more often than needed. Most of the men are left alone in that way compared to the women, but once in a while, Marcus feels the need to exert his power. He's also smart, and I think he lets some of them ... uh, take his place. I'm not really sure, maybe there's more to it than that. So most of them are actually on his side, but a couple are definitely not. I can

talk to them too. This is dangerous though. The back door is guarded, all day and night."

"Do you think you can talk to all the people and arrange it so that the door is guarded by one of the ones you trust? We want to go tonight, but we're going to have to be quick and quiet."

"Yes, I can, and that's a good idea. I'll do that during the day, talk to all of them." Kuniko stops speaking and just looks at Eve, a single tear welling up in her bruised eye. Suddenly, she hugs Eve, and a muffled "Thank you" comes out mixed with a sob. Just as quickly, she releases Eve and walks down the stairs, Eve trailing her, and leaves after collecting the empty pot.

Eve watches her disappear, anxiety building, but mixed with hope. They're going to help these people, and now she has an ally.

***

The rest of the day trudges by like the deliberate tick of a clock on the day before vacation. Eve and Amy busy themselves around the house, pretending they're staying there and doing what they can to make it their own, just to kill time before dark. The curtains in the room where they'd slept are threadbare, and so they swap some from another room. They then sweep the hardwood floors on the ground floor, clean the windows, and manage to wrap up the rest of their chores by early evening. The rain petered out late in the afternoon, leaving sullen clouds drifting by quickly as the front is blown away by whatever weather is coming next.

Eve is startled when she hears a knock on the door, followed by the sound of it opening and an unfamiliar voice calling from downstairs, "Anyone home? It's time for dinner."

"We'll be right down!"

They bustle down to the kitchen to find a short man in his early thirties leaning against the counter. He's slim but muscular in the manner of someone who made his living outdoors, and the last of his fair, blond hair is cropped short in a military cut. He introduces himself as Aaron, with a kind smile, and tells them since the rain has stopped, they're all going to dine together outdoors. It's one of Marcus's traditions, he explains, that they all have their meals in a group whenever possible to promote togetherness. Eve suspects it's also so he can keep an eye on his flock and prevent some of the inevitable whispering that must occur here.

As they walk across the interior of the compound, Aaron says to them in a low voice, "I talked to Kuniko."

"Okay," Eve answers as casually as she can.

"I'll be the guard tonight at the rear exit. I don't usually get that duty, but I swapped out with Vince, who hates being inside and sitting still, so he was happy enough to trade for wall duty where he can walk around. How many people are coming to get us?"

"Two. A brother and sister."

"Two? That's it? I hope that's enough, though Kuniko told me she's spoken to at least a half-dozen people."

"That's good." Eve feels a tiny surge of optimism. Aaron looks capable enough, and having Vince farther away from them seems like a plus. She just hopes Kuniko has gotten to everyone she wanted to, and their numbers will be enough in case things don't go smoothly.

They reach the tables and find seats in the middle of one of them. Marcus calls the group to order with the tap of a spoon against his glass. "Everyone, I have happy news. Eve and Amy have agreed to join us here, in safety. I hope you all are as pleased as I am for their company. I'd like each of you to introduce yourselves now, maybe a little backstory for what you did in the old days." He smiles broadly at his people as he moves smoothly among the tables, confident in his power but making gestures of welcome and comfort as he circulates. A hand on a shoulder here, a private smile there. His charisma is undeniable, and once more, Eve feels the renewed surge of anger that he could offer so much but feels it's acceptable to expect something so personal in return.

Kuniko moves between the tables, too, delivering food along with another woman. As people greet Eve and Amy and give their names, Kuniko pauses and ensures Eve can see her. Each time, Kuniko gives an imperceptible nod or shake of her head toward whoever is introducing themselves. It's so subtle, Eve misses the first few signals before understanding. Then she watches closely. Maya, Emily, Lisa Ann, Bob, Victoria-but-I-go-by-Vicky are all nods. So five women and two men, counting Kuniko and Aaron. *The truck will be cozy but enough*, she thinks, but they could probably find another running vehicle once they're clear of the danger so no one will have to ride in the bed during the long trip back to New York.

The meal goes by quickly with the quiet hubbub of a group chatting about the day, glad for the end of the rain since it makes for idle days here and pleased for the clearer weather that's likely for tomorrow. She hears no comments about zombies, no discussion of the conditions here, but she sees some fleeting smiles from the people Kuniko spoke to, and she feels good. They're going to offer these people something they clearly need: hope.

As dinner winds down, Marcus makes his way to their table and rests his big hands on Amy's shoulders. He asks if he could speak to Eve privately for a moment, and Eve sees many pairs of eyes dart toward her. It isn't as if Eve could refuse, so she stands up and walks into the ever-growing dusk toward a small clutch of trees with the big man.

Once they're far enough away from the group, Marcus turns toward her with a grin. "I'm looking forward to tomorrow night, Eve. You will be most welcome here."

"I don't know what to say." Eve struggles again with an impassive expression, unsure what facade to put on. She's frightened of what could happen here if they're unable to escape, yet anxiously excited at getting away and being able to take some people with them.

"You don't have to say anything. I actually prefer it that way, though Vince is of a different opinion. Perhaps you'll find out after a time, though I find myself drawn to you, so he may have to be more patient than he'd like."

Her meal threatens to boil out of her stomach. He's so frank and direct about this horrible arrangement, such clear entitlement to the tribute he feels he's due. Part of her wants to kill him, though she has yet to take a life, even a zombie one, but she's repulsed to her core by this man, his words, and his actions.

"Have a nice night. Sleep well since you may not do so much tomorrow," he adds with a wink and a chuckle, of all things. Then he walks away, leaving her alone with her thoughts.

Their plan had better work.

***

Their plan relies on the moon for their clock, so Eve is thankful that the skies are now clear as she walks back to the house, flanked by Kuniko and Amy. Others are nearby and winding their own way back to their dwellings, so they speak quietly. "I got to almost everyone I wanted to," Kuniko says. "Everyone I can trust."

"Aaron told me he was going to be the guard tonight. That's good."

"Yes, he's a good man. He tries to be a peacekeeper of sorts, steering Vince away from people when he can if he's lost his temper. He's been kind to me after ... well, after *that*. Vince is really the bad one. He's violent and always angry, even during normal days. He takes advantage of his position and knows no one can fight back, not here, or it's just worse for them the next time. He's really dangerous and unpredictable, Eve."

Eve can hear the fear in the petite woman's voice. "We're going to get out of here. They," she says, referring to the siblings outside, "will meet us at the door when the moon is dead overhead, then we'll all slip out and be gone before they know it. You need to get back around to the ones you talked to and tell them to be there, or they'll get left behind. And to be quiet."

"I know. I will. See you soon." Kuniko fades off into the dark as they reach the front door.

The landscaping lights strewn around provide enough illumination for them to see the handle clearly, and she and Amy duck inside and lock it behind them.

"I'm still scared," Amy says.

"Me too, but we're going to be okay. You know how strong they are. Think back to the lake. There were, what, forty or fifty zombies? And they killed *all* of them. Even if something goes wrong, there aren't going to be nearly that many people to fight, and all we have to do is run to the truck and get out of here. It's going to be fine. You have to have faith." She hugs the girl tight, smelling her hair and feeling protective to the point she knows she'll sacrifice her own life to save Amy's. "Let's go upstairs and get your backpack ready, make sure you have all your stuff." She needs to keep them occupied for a couple of hours, and while there isn't going to be much to fill the time, this is better than nothing.

***

It takes us about an hour to get ready. We arm ourselves with everything that seems practical but don't carry anything that's going to make noise or slow us down. Taking soot from the fireplace again, we darken our hands and faces to go with our dark clothing. Guns bristle from my sister in every direction, though she's disappointed she doesn't have her Bo with her too. We forgot it back in the bed of the truck, and she's insistent about retrieving it, so since we have time to occupy, I agree to make the detour since I know she won't let it go. Scant cloud cover allows the rising moon to light our way as we walk through the abandoned streets with the dogs. There's no need to rush as we have roughly two more hours until we're going to make our approach, so we stroll at an easy pace while keeping our eyes and ears open.

Before making the one turn marked by a dormant fast-food restaurant on the opposite corner (no more billions served), the dogs freeze, noses pointing upwind. We halt, seeing nothing at first, but then a small crowd drifts into moonlit view at the intersection a block away. Maybe a dozen or more zombies deliberately walking toward the madcap building's front entrance. Sinking back into the shadows between two houses, pulling the dogs with us, we watch them pass and wait a few more minutes to ensure they're gone, and we have remained unnoticed.

"Do you think that was the same pack as last night?" Morgan asks.

"Probably. I wonder if the fort draws them here, if they can smell dinner inside, and that's why they stick around. Kind of like they're all safe inside the walls, but the walls also keep them in danger. We're gonna have to keep an eye out on the way back."

We get to the house that holds our getaway vehicle. The piece of firewood is still resting against the door, so all is clear. Morgan ducks inside to get the Bo and confirms one more time that the keys are in the ignition and ready to go. It's time.

"I still think we need to leave the dogs in house number two," I say. "Much as I want to have them with us, if they bark all of a sudden, we're going to be in deep shit. It'll only take a minute to collect them on the way back since the house is on the way here." I know the dogs will be unhappy about being left behind, but tonight's work relies heavily on silence.

"Agreed, though they'll be mad at you."

"I'll give them a shitload of dog biscuits after to make up for it, or maybe some steak or something. One of these days, we need to find them some companionship too, some girl dogs. Puppies would be fun, and we can't have too many guard dogs."

"Good idea, though Ajax might still take a shit in your shoes."

I laugh at that and feel good. We have a good plan, we're well armed, we're good at being quiet, and we trust Eve has figured out a way to get people to the back door so we can sneak out without any fuss.

The trip back to house two takes about thirty minutes as we're going cautiously, thanks to the pack of zombies from earlier. We bring the dogs inside, hand them a few biscuits, and duck back outside into the cooling night. I can hear them quietly whining from inside for a minute and then hear them move away from the door. Go there quietly, open the door, grab the people, scoot back here for the dogs, run to the truck, and get the hell out of town.

Simple.

***

Morgan and I make our way to our destination without incident. We keep to the shadows and creep in a two-block radius just like we did the night before, until diverting toward the back wall. Not a sound from either of us, and we leapfrog our way over the last hundred yards, one watching, one moving. Eve is supposed to have arranged for one light in the escape house, and we see a dull red glow in the low corner of a window on the ground floor of the house, right in the middle of the back wall. I glance up at the moon and see it's straight overhead, and so we make our final approach, hugging tight to the walls. We aren't going to knock, no need to make noise. We're just supposed to be ready for the door to open, and if it doesn't, we're going to wait as long as it takes.

CHAPTER 10

E ve has been watching the moon from their bedroom window, listening to Amy's steady breathing as she takes a nap. She's amazed the child is able to sleep through the wait; Eve's own heart is racing, and her thoughts are ablaze with what-ifs. Excitement if they escape, terror about what will happen if they're captured, all of it a big, anxious, emotional soup roiling her stomach.

When the light of the moon says it's time, she gently nudges the youngster awake, and they collect their backpacks and carefully go downstairs. Rather than go out the front door and risk being seen, they go into a ground-floor bedroom that faces the side yard and step through a window into the darkness.

It's eerily quiet.

Sticking to the shadows, they ease across two lawns to reach the middle house and tap at the front door. Fortunately, the front of this house is completely shaded by a mammoth tree in the front yard. Eve holds her breath, trying madly to figure out a cover story in case it isn't a friend who opens the door. She releases her breath when Kuniko's pale face greets them, and she ushers them quickly inside. Eve can sense several other bodies in the inky darkness but can't make out how many or who, and hopes it's all seven that Eve counted up during dinner. Whispered instructions are passed around, and they file noiselessly through the foyer and kitchen and then to the rear door. A male voice somewhere ahead of them asks, "Okay?" and she hears the click of two dead bolts and then the latch being released. They're fully outside, and she looks around quickly in the faint moonlight.

"Eve!" comes a hushed call.

She stares in the direction it came from and makes out the two forms of her companions against the wall a few feet away. Her heart races but with happiness this time. *We're out*, she thinks, *we're going to be safe in just a few minutes.*

She's horribly wrong.

Blinding light erupts from every direction. Atop the walls, from several of the nearby trees, glaring and cutting through the night. All of them are thrown into sharp relief, and Eve holds her hands up to shield her eyes, but it's no use.

"Well, well, well. What do we have here?"

Marcus.

***

I freeze in place, as does Morgan beside me. We're completely exposed. The area is as well lit as a megastore parking lot at Christmas. I immediately draw both of my .45s and point them at the man who could only be Marcus, but he simply laughs and steps closer, allowing a clear view of the dozen armed men and women behind him as they step from the shadows. We've outsmarted ourselves. If I'd brought the dogs, they'd have smelled all these people hiding in wait for us.

"Drop the weapons, all of them," Marcus says as he strolls over to Eve and holds a pistol to her head. "I'm not going to ask twice. I do like Eve and look forward to getting to know her *much* more intimately, but I have no compunction about shooting her at all."

Shit. I've always hated this moment in movies, when the bad guys get the drop on the good guys and order them to drop their weapons while holding someone hostage. The good guys almost always do, though it means that instead of the one person dying and everyone else having a chance to escape, no one has a chance when disarmed. But, I raise my hands up in a placating move and then crouch to set my handguns on the ground at my feet. I unsling the shotgun from my back and place it on the ground as well, and then I remove the KNIFE from its sheath and drop it point-first into the turf. I have a heavy-duty LED flashlight in the pocket of my cargo pants, but I don't bother with that. Morgan does the same, dropping her pistol, rifle, and Bo. I can practically feel her seething with anger and hope she isn't going to do anything rash, but we're really, really badly outnumbered, so maybe rash is a good idea.

"Welcome back, Morgan," Marcus says with a grin as he lowers his gun, now that we're disarmed, but keeps a hand on Eve's arm. "I'd so hoped you'd rejoin us at some point. Vince did too. Where is his dog, by the way? And did you notice we found Jack after all? It was nice of you to back your car up toward us out of caution when you visited. That lovely Corvette had dealership decals on the rear panel, so we knew you'd come from Denver. It was easy enough to send the boys out to find him and bring him back. He died screaming you know, since we hung him on the wall alive at first but within reach of the zombies. That's why they seem to come by every evening now, to see if there is someone new to nibble."

Morgan cries out in anguish, the first time I've ever heard her do so. She had a soft spot for the lunatic who'd believed he was a pirate and had escaped from here. When they met, he told her about the place and Marcus and warned her to stay away from there. Morgan being Morgan, however, she ignored his warning and drove here to see everything for herself.

Marcus turns his gaze toward me. "And who might you be? A boyfriend? To Eve? To Morgan? To both of them in these heady days?"

I don't reply to his taunts, just stand there. I'm counting bad guys and odds and coming up way short. We're in deep shit, and all I can hope for is they don't kill us outright. Given that Marcus probably wants some revenge on my sister, I figure she'll be spared for a bit, but I'm not so sure about my chances. Maybe it would be better if they did kill us rather than keep anyone for entertainment.

When I don't respond, Marcus just shrugs and says, "No matter. Search them, all of them. And carefully this time."

Vince grimaces at the insulting reminder, hands his shotgun to the man to his left, and walks to each of the escapees. None of them have weapons, though one woman is relieved of a pair of brilliant-red knitting needles that look like they could do some damage. He finishes with them and then moves over to Morgan. "I've been waiting a long time for this, bitch," he snarls.

"For what? Someone who wasn't afraid of you? Guess there's a first time for everything, even for a muscle-bound, thick-skulled Neanderthal like you that's only learned a couple handfuls of things along the way, like how to use the invention called a fork instead of your fingers for eating. Have you figured out that white stuff near the toilets yet? The paper circles on cardboard tubes in brackets on the wall?" I'm not sure why Morgan is baiting him, but it's one of her skills.

"No, for this, you smart-mouthy whore." He grabs at Morgan's chest, hard, squeezing her and twisting his huge hands until she gasps but doesn't cry out. She isn't going to give him the satisfaction, and I'm about to lunge at him when Marcus notices and swings his pistol back against Eve's temple, looking at me in warning. "And for this." He punches her in the crotch, and she goes down in a heap. "You'll learn to be scared of me. Everyone does."

I'm shocked and frankly thunderstruck. I've never seen someone do that to a woman before.

He laughs cruelly, steps over her prone body, and stops in front of me. "How about you, tough guy? Afraid of me yet?"

"Nope. You're just one big dumb piece of shit who just picked a fight with the wrong people. You're going to be sorry you did that." My words sound brave, but I know we're in big trouble, and I can't see a way out. A sharp bark sounds from a few streets away, but I don't pay much attention since I'm staring at his cleft chin just a few inches away from my eyes and deciding whether I ought to try and headbutt him.

Before I get the chance, he punches me in the balls. He's fast. And strong, dammit.

Every guy would like to think he can take a shot in the nuts and keep standing. Every guy is totally wrong, especially when the blow is delivered by a man flirting with 250 pounds. I see stars, feel stunning, crippling nausea, and am glad I didn't eat dinner—he'd be wearing it right about now. I drop to my knees, gasping for air and clutching the beans. The pain is awful, worse even than the zombie bite. The ground looms up at me, and I fight to stay conscious.

Did you just say "beans"? That's close, but they're not that small! Not going to be using those anytime soon, are we? Not that it matters because you're screwed anyway! Well, wait, not screwed since your nuts are gonna be the size of grapefruits in a minute, so screwing isn't going to happen. You're fucked, that's it. No, that's not it either. Oh, never mind.

Really? Now?

"Anyone else want to run their mouth?" Vince shouts as he glares at the crowd, looking from face to face, indifferent to whether they're insiders or those trying to leave. He's just looking for a conflict to vent his anger on.

Marcus interrupts. "Indoors, *now*, everyone. No stupid moves."

The armed squad splits into two groups—several go into the house first to prevent anyone from running away,

I suppose, and the bulk of them trail our now-miserable group of captives. Two of the other women from "their" side yank Morgan to her feet and carry her through the house. One of our captors gathers up our weapons. Eleven of us against roughly a dozen of them, which wouldn't have been the worst odds I've faced except that none of us are armed at this point.

As I emerge from the inside door, stumbling thanks to the pain and struggling to stay upright without help, I hear another faint bark from outside the walls, which makes me curse my stupidity again for leaving the dogs in the house. My balls are aching, no surprise there, but we have much bigger problems. This has gone so far sideways that I can't see a way out, not even one where I can kill "my" people to spare them what's surely coming at the hands of Marcus and his minions. I have no weapons, we're wildly outnumbered, and while I intend to fight when and if I can, I think we're sunk, and a small part of me despairs at the thought.

After we go through the house and enter the interior of the compound, lights snap on inside as well, from fixtures on the upper corners of several houses, while those outside click sharply off. We're surrounded by Marcus and his people, trapped in the center of a loose circle. The guy carrying our gear drops everything haphazardly in a heap outside their line.

I have no ideas on how to escape this mess, and I can tell Morgan doesn't either, though from the fury of her expression, it's obvious she wants a fight despite her own pain. Marcus releases his grasp on Eve and pushes her back to our crowd. She staggers toward me, and I catch her arms and look at her for a moment, trying to send some measure of unspoken comfort, but I don't think I'm very convincing. It sure doesn't look like it from the barely contained panic that's written across her face.

"Ah, so a boyfriend of Eve, and now that I get a clearer look at you, perhaps a sibling of the fiery Morgan. Is that right? I think it is. Thank you, Aaron. You may rejoin us."

A shorter man steps out of the middle of the captives and into the outer circle. I hear Eve gasp and understand immediately that she's been tricked somehow by this man. A slender woman behind her, with dark hair pulled back from her pretty face, also brings her hand up to her mouth, astonishment and betrayal writ strong on her features.

"And here we are. I'll tell you, it was a close thing. I wanted to believe that our new guests were nothing more than they said they were, just hopeful travelers stranded and in need of accommodations. But one thing in particular stood out. You both," he says with a nod toward Eve and Amy, "looked too comfortable to have been on the road and on your own for a long period of time. Not really dirty, though you had some smudges on your faces, your clothes are in good shape, none of the unavoidable stress of these fine times showing on your faces. So we watched, and given some recent suspicion of my dear Kuniko following Morgan's first visit, observed her circulating for too long after bringing you some food. Then it was simple to push Aaron into your confidence, and now we've got our little midnight soiree. So, why are you here? To 'rescue' people, I presume? Tut, tut. I think we'll keep

Eve, Amy, and Morgan. We have some unfinished business of assorted variety. You," he says as he swings his gaze my way again, "are probably not going to be very fortunate. I apologize in advance, but you appear to be rather capable and, therefore, would be a risk to keep around, so you must go." He then addresses the crowd of attempted escapees. "Those of you who were attempting to leave, you will be punished. I think we'll be giving old Jack some company on the wall."

A series of successive barks sound, and this time, I pay closer attention. It's from two different dogs, so it must be Ajax and Jack. I wonder how they got out of the house, and what they're barking at, but it probably doesn't make a difference. Even if they get in here to help us somehow, we're unarmed, outnumbered, and they're just dogs. Vince's ears perk up, however, and I realize he must have recognized Jack's bark.

Morgan goes back down to the ground with a groan and gestures for Amy to come over to her. No one moves to stop her, and I watch Amy unsling her backpack, unzip it, and lay it on the ground near my sister as she crouches down. Amy's form blocks Morgan from anyone's line of sight, but I can see her hand snake its way into the pack, probably searching for the pistol we'd hidden at the bottom, wrapped in a sweatshirt, before we sent them in. We'd hoped then that any searches would have overlooked an early teen and her possessions, and I hope now that we were right. One gun isn't going to level the odds, but it's better than no guns, and maybe it will allow us to reclaim those weapons that have been taken from us. I have no idea what Marcus is going to do, whether shoot us all right here, save some of them for punishment (amusement), or something in the middle, but I don't intend to go down without a fight.

More barking. A lot more barking, and now it's coming with the challenging bellow I know is from Ajax. Something is brewing outside the walls, over by the front door protected by the armored bus.

"What's all that noise?" asks one of the men in Marcus's pack. "We don't have any dogs, not since she took Vince's last time."

"Did you bring Oliver back with you?" This comes from Vince in a surprisingly different voice than the one he used to "greet" us and challenge the crowd. It's the voice of a boy who lost his dog, a voice of longing and sorrow.

I remember the first dog I lost, Irving; my wingman who'd followed me everywhere and protected me once from a copperhead by cornering the snake against a rock while I moved away. I miss that dog, and for a scant moment, I feel a twinge of sympathy for Vince. Just a twinge, though that also might have been the flashes of pain still radiating from my balls.

More barking. "Ollie? Ollie, is that you, boy?" Vince moves rapidly away from the crowd before anyone else can say or do anything and jogs quickly toward the bus.

No one moves to stop him; the rest of them stand guard over us as he clambers through the open wing doors and up into the driver's seat and turns the key. I risk a glance at my sister, who holds her arm inside Amy's backpack and gives me a small nod. One gun, a flashlight, and desperation is what we have, that and maybe a pair of badass dogs in a minute.

The bus is parked inside the walls across the opening to the outside world, with the front and rear of it overlapping the cinder-block walls between houses. The driver would have no view of what's outside unless he's cautious enough to go to the middle of the vehicle and look through the barred windows first. Vince does no such thing but instead just fires it up and begins to drive forward.

Just as the rear bumper is about to clear the entrance, I put two and two together and immediately scream at the top of my lungs, "*No! Stop!* Stop him!" I try to sprint to the bus, but the flaring pain between my legs is too much, it's too far, and he can't hear me over the rattle of the diesel engine anyway. I swing back to face the crowd of people and howl in warning to all of them, "Run! For the love of God, *run!*"

For outside the door Vince has just opened wide enough to look for his lost dog is a massive horde of zombies. Morgan and I saw a couple dozen of them in our scouting and approach, and while we thought they were the same group winding their way back around, they weren't. The floodlights' illumination doesn't reach all the way out beyond the walls and so only lights the first few ranks of monsters closing in on our dogs, who've backed up to the bus and are challenging the zombies as they try to warn us of the coming danger. I count roughly forty quickly and can see vague shapes extending well into the darkness beyond.

There's far more than I want to try and count, or fight. They must've been gathering for an assault on the high walls and the residents inside, and now we're caught in the middle with one goddamn gun.

Live sporting events of any size had been a thrill in the days gone by. Seeing it all in person was the best way to watch it. There was nothing like it that the big-screen televisions and surround-sound systems at home could adequately capture. Tens of thousands of people, all engaged in watching their gladiators compete, and the abrupt victorious roar of the crowd at a winning three-point shot, late-inning home run, or bone-crunching tackle to save a touchdown was a miraculous thing to experience as the sound rushed over you.

Muuuuuuuuhhhhh!

This was not a sound I wanted to hear in person.

Louder than I have ever heard it before, the terrifying attack call of the zombies. It rolls over us with the inexorable promise of a slow and painful death in its echoes. The most I've ever faced is the group of about fifty Ned had brought to kill us all out of jealousy over my connection with Eve. This is many, *many* more than fifty mouths uttering their cry of conquest, and they pour through the gap in a horrid flood of flailing limbs, gaping mouths, and grasping hands, chasing the dogs who have wisely hauled ass inside as soon as there's space.

And right there in the middle of the flood is yet another alpha zombie. It's impossible to mistake her for anything else. She's magnificent in a terrible way, nearly six feet tall

with dyed magenta hair shorn in a buzz cut, and broad shoulders poking out from a turquoise tank top. She waves her hands in all directions, dispersing her army of the dead to go wreak havoc and swell the ranks of the deceased.

I spin from where I'd stopped about halfway between the group of people and the now-open door and look at the dumbstruck crowd of people who're about to die. Eve and Amy stand among the five women and one man in the captives crowd, and Morgan is already moving toward the pile of our weapons, pistol in hand. Marcus and his minions are frozen in place, shocked by the waves of zombies now trapping everyone inside a killing zone of cinder-block walls and suburban houses.

I run.

We need weapons and speed now. No fighting, not unless it's to clear a path, just running. I race to my friends and sister so I can have them close to me and protect them. The terrible thought that I should save a few rounds at the end if we're surrounded, to spare us the horror of being alive as we're eaten, dances across my mind, and I slip one of the clips for the .45 into a back pocket for a just-in-case scenario as I run.

Ajax and Jack barrel past me, sprinting to the group of humans who finally scatter in all directions, like bowling pins that have been sent sprawling. My group has stayed together with the other captives, and my heart sinks a little. A small group has a better chance of avoiding and escaping, but there are ten of us, and that's too many to escape notice by the cadre of creatures running and stumbling across the open space, looking for a meal. I want to help these new people, I really do, but my focus is on my three.

A man darts in front of me, the other main guard, somehow deciding to fight humans instead of zombies, and I level him with a flying tackle that would have made a pro football coach proud. His rifle explodes out of his hands and skitters across the asphalt, and I scrabble on all fours to get it, turning to look over my shoulder as I stand. Easily over a hundred are inside the walls by now and fanning out to chase the scattering people, but the gate is now mostly clear. I fire once, twice, three times into the pack heading our way, watch two monsters drop, and then curse as the gun clicks empty. What kind of idiot only has three rounds these days? I throw the gun to the ground and then change my mind since it'll at least serve as a club, so I scoop it back up and run. More gunfire erupts from all directions—pistols, rifles, and shotguns all flash from the shadowy corners unlit by the floodlights. The fallen guard behind me goes under a pile of zombies, and they begin to devour him. His cries are bloodcurdling and awful, spurring me to greater speed.

The screams start from elsewhere too. Howling, ululating shrieks echo off the walls as the zombies hit home and begin to find victims, and I try to shut out the sounds as I reach our group, including the "new" people. Some of them stand still like sheep, stupidly watching the rest of the herd be slaughtered, and I spark them to motion. "Run! Goddammit, *run*! Get out the back door! Fucking *move*!"

"We can't!" says Kuniko, panic dancing in her voice. "It's got a keyed dead bolt, and I saw Marcus lock it and remove the key when they brought us in."

Shit. That leaves the front door, which is over a hundred yards away now but vacant of invaders at this point, so it's the only idea we have left. Morgan tosses my pistols to me one by one, and then the shotgun. I scoop my KNIFE up and hand it to one of the other women, hand the shotgun to a bald-headed man with a spectacular biker's goatee, and press one of my .45s into Eve's unwilling hand. Morgan similarly distributes her weapons, keeping only her Bo and a pistol for herself. This is a debacle, but we may have a chance. None of our former captors are in view now, though the dwindling muzzle flashes and concussions from around the compound show where there are fewer of them remaining.

"Toward the walls, everyone. Move!" I command, running through them as my idea takes shape. If we can skirt the walls, largely in the unlit shadows, maybe we can reach the front door and get out, get back to the truck, and get the hell away. The rustle of the crowd tells me I have followers, and Ajax comes to run at my side as I lead the way.

It works, mostly. We're less than fifty feet from escaping when a pack of zombies sees us and blocks the way, standing in a seething battle line across the remaining space. There are more of them than us, and their call attracts others, who begin to stream in our direction from the far corners of the sanctuary-turned-charnel house.

Muuuuuuuhhhhh!

"*Fight!*" Morgan screams. "Fight but run your way through!" And then she plunges first into the fray, a whirling mass of muscle and wood, laying waste around her like a Middle Ages warrior.

I pick two zombies off from the fringes, and then the lines close in a writhing mess. It's too close an area to fire guns for fear of hitting one of our people, but then I realize it doesn't matter. Some of us are going to die here, and only by surrendering completely to the battle are any of us going to escape. So I begin to shoot in the direction of the opening, focusing shots on a narrow span, trusting my instincts, and picking more of the monsters off.

Yawning mouths loom into view and vanish in a spray of blood and fire, scrabbling fingers with ragged nails scrape across my arms and neck and drop away when my pistol shot vaporizes a horrible face. Screams come from close by, and I see one of the new people go under a mass of flailing limbs, howling for help as she goes completely out of sight. I can't save her, not with five of them on top of her already, so I fire a few shots into the pile and hope one of them made it through to bring her mercy.

I spin back toward the gate and see Eve surrounded by three more of them, two females and a male circling her and looking for an opening. She holds the pistol I've given her out at arm's length, shakily, and pivots to face each of them whenever one darts forward.

"Shoot, Eve!" I yell at the top of my lungs above the maelstrom as I run in her direction. "Shoot, goddammit!"

She finally fires, blowing one of them away to the side, but drops the gun with a small cry.

I reach her side just in time, shoot the other two, scoop up her gun, and press it hard into her hand. "You have to do this. As many times as it takes for us to get out of here. Just shoot. Don't think!"

She nods numbly, and we keep moving toward the exit.

More screams, more gunshots, and then suddenly, we're through them and racing for the exit. Seven of us left, bodies of both kinds strewn in all directions in our wake, some moving, most of them still. Morgan, Eve, and Amy are there, along with the biker guy, Kuniko, and one other woman. All of us are spattered in blood, bathed in sweat, and breathing heavily. Ajax and Jack snarl at the approaching second wave of zombies now less than fifty feet away, baring their bloody maws and unafraid to wreak further carnage.

We run toward freedom … so close by.

And then we stop after just a handful of steps.

Vince emerges from the sheltering bulk of the bus, stepping down from inside and blocking the freedom beyond the walls. He holds his shotgun shakily toward us, still unable to figure out which side he's supposed to be on, stupidly determined to fight the people instead of the undead, just like the other guard. What the fuck is wrong with these guys?

"Take me with you," he pleads, surprising me yet again. "You have to, or I'll shoot. Get me out of here!"

The big man is panicked, terrified of being on the other end of pain for a change, and threatens our escape with his fear. He doesn't want to go with us; he just wants to use us to help him escape. His eyes are wide and dart in every direction, across our group and then over our shoulders to see our pursuers.

"I don't think so," says Morgan, and she suddenly raises her pistol and shoots him rather casually in the face.

He drops in a heap, gore leaking out the back of his skull into a spreading puddle of crimson. She steps over his body to pick up the now-ownerless gun, racks the slide, turns back to us, and tosses it to the woman I don't know.

"Let's go," Morgan says simply as Vince's body twitches at her feet.

Now, we really run. Biker Guy slows us down a bit. It seems he's injured, either from the fight or something else, since he runs with a limping gait, favoring his left leg. But we make it clear of the walls and the flaring light from inside the compound. Out into the open streets that cloak us in ebony, until I remember I still have the flashlight and flick it on so we'll have something to follow. The light dances across the road, illuminating trees, shrubs, cars, and abandoned toys as we flee. Our pursuers eventually lose interest as far as I can tell; it's a small blessing that zombies seem to lose the ability to really run any faster than a human jog. Besides, their easy dinner is trapped inside, just waiting to be caught, and no predator likes to work too hard for their food.

We stumble to a halt in the backyard of our forward house on achy legs flooded with adrenaline, and I see how the dogs must've gotten out, and ultimately saved us. There's a dog door up on the second-floor deck we'd overlooked, luckily.

Morgan turns to me, her sweaty face lit by the flashlight's cast, blood that I hope isn't hers streaked across her left cheek. All of us bear the residue of the battle, with scrapes here and there, but no one seems seriously banged up.

"We just need to go," Morgan says. "Keep going. There's nothing inside that we need since the dogs got out on their own. We can get more food on the way, water too. It's time to leave."

I agree, and we keep moving, winding our way through the streets as quietly as a group of seven humans and two dogs can. We don't come across anything on the way but jump at every noise and nearly blow a pair of squirrels into oblivion as they jump from tree to tree. We finally reach and turn at the fast-food place. After another minute, we get to the house holding our truck. The firewood piece is in place, so I duck inside, slide the garage door up and out of the way, and fire up the truck, rolling it into the driveway. Everyone piles in, my original group in the cab and our three newcomers in the bed with the dogs.

It's indeed time to go.

We haven't saved as many people as we wanted to, but the building of falsehood and mistreatment is ended, Vince is dead, and everyone else on Marcus's team has likely been slaughtered inside the confining walls that once protected them and their dark secrets. We move steadily out of the garage and down the street, the high beams of the truck illuminating the way to the rest of our escape. Everyone keeps watch in case something jumps out of the shadows, and we see nothing for a few blocks until a big man comes into view. Right behind him is the alpha, doggedly pursuing him. The man is limping along, blood sheeting his right leg, and his clothes are torn and hair is mussed with a large patch of it missing. He glances desperately over his shoulder as the truck's lights bathe him in their implacable glow.

It's Marcus.

The alpha spins around to snarl at us as Marcus hobbles to a stop, turns to us, and raises his arms weakly to the side like he had in greeting, though now in supplication.

I coast the truck to a stop about fifty feet from them and look around the interior of the truck.

"What do we want to do?" I ask. "He's a person, and he's hurt. Leave him here to let him take his chances, or kill the alpha and bring him with us? Kill him?"

I hate the idea of a cold-blooded killing, but there's a Southern phrase I've heard over the years, half in jest, about a simple defense against murder charges: "He needed killin'." It seems to fit well here, but I'm inclined to just leave him. There's no way he'll ever threaten us again from twelve hundred miles away, and I say so to the group. There's a little symmetry too—bad guy meets bad end.

Morgan disagrees. "True, he won't threaten us, and yeah, he'll probably die here, but what if he doesn't? What if he lives and does it all over again to other innocent people? And we probably should kill her too. One less monster is good math."

I look at Eve, who shakes her head, either unsure of what to do or unhappy at the idea of killing him or leaving him to let fate sort it out. I'm not surprised and turn to look at Amy too. "I think we should leave him," she says, "but I hope he dies. I heard what he said to you yesterday, Eve, even though you thought I was sleeping. I can be sneaky when I need to, used to have to be that way in the foster houses. I was at the top of the stairs and heard everything. What he was saying, that's just disgusting and wrong." She speaks vehemently, and I wonder just what Marcus had said to elicit such a strong response from a kid.

Eve doesn't even react to Amy's confession to eavesdropping, which is a surprise, but she's probably still dealing with the trauma of the fight. It was her first time pulling the trigger after all. Zombie or not, consciously deciding to kill is a bigger deal than characters in movies and books would have you believe. If there is a pot of gold at the end of it, it's that killing your second zombie is much, *much* easier.

We're apparently leaning toward just driving past him like a hitchhiker stuck on the highway, when there's a tap against the back glass. It's Kuniko. She hops down over the lip of the bed, comes to my window, and leans in. "A pistol, please. I know you're talking about what to do, the decent thing or less decent. It's not your decision." There's something on her face, a determined stare that masks a great deal of pain, that makes me wordlessly hand over one of my .45s. She thanks me quietly and marches off into the white light of the headlights toward Marcus.

The alpha has turned away from the truck and is closing in on him as well, arms raised, fingers curled into claws, and I'm tempted to call Kuniko back and just let things happen, but I don't. We sit there in the idling truck as she walks up to them. I'm surprised at how comfortable she is with the gun. She brings it smoothly to firing position as she walks and blows the zombie's head off in a spectacular spatter of brain, bone, and blood that fans out into the evening air and then mists away in the glare of the headlights.

She reaches Marcus and begins talking, though we can't hear anything. It's a short, though animated conversation. She points the gun at him and says something else, and he drops awkwardly to his knees in the street with his hands out in front of him, clearly imploring her for what must be mercy. He speaks nonstop for a minute, and I check the rearview mirrors while we wait, a little concerned we aren't as clear of danger as I would like. I hear a second gunshot and turn my attention forward to see Marcus's body topple to the ground. Kuniko steps closer, fires downward again into his prone form, and then walks calmly back to us.

Kuniko stops at my open window again and hands the gun back to me, butt first. Her face is impassive, and she speaks in a monotone voice. "I told him to beg. To beg like he forced me to, every time. To not do it. To convince me he deserved to live and have a second chance. That everything he did to me, to all of them, wasn't terrible enough to take his life. He didn't convince me."

She climbs back into the truck without another word, I drop it into drive, and we head back toward New York, leaving all the chapters of horror of the place behind us. Toward the real sanctuary ... the one that needs no title.

CHAPTER 11

We barely stop on the way back. Bathroom breaks, when needed, at gas stops in grim towns that are devoid of everything and everyone who once made their way through the world in the past, before being swept into darkness by the bellicose monsters walking the Earth. Twelve hundred miles is a long drive in any era, and we're all exhausted by the trip, the intensity of the drama within the walls, and the battle for escape. We drive more slowly, too, since our new people are in the bed, and the weather is cooler than normal for this time of year. No one speaks much, just piping up when a pit stop is needed. All of us are lost in our thoughts, and I admit I'm troubled by the two executions I've just witnessed. Not by the outcome since both were deserved, but by what had pushed both women to that.

I witnessed what Vince had done to Morgan, and knowing my sister's black-and-white outlook on the world even before all of this, I'm not all that stunned. She has the steel inside her to make quick, hard (and often impulsive) decisions. While that has gotten her in trouble in the past, it serves her well now.

Kuniko is an unknown beyond what we understand of the suffering of the people who were held hostage by fear in Marcus's building, and I try to force my mind away from what Marcus and his sidekicks had done to the residents—the curse of an active imagination paired with the experiences from the chapters of our story with asshole Jack, the three men who "greeted" my first group when we'd arrived in New York, and Ned's incredible betrayal. People have done a pretty good job of being lousy to one another before, but the new world seems to encourage some of the shit to rise to the top of the heap. Our home isn't going to be that way, but I ponder how we'll absorb our new folks, and what three more faces will mean. I'm disappointed, too, that we lost so many of them on the way out, but I'm relieved our original group is unharmed and intact. Having lost my people before, I'm not sure my psyche would survive any more deaths.

***

And finally, we're home.

I turn the truck into the driveway, past the gate, and guide it down the shady, rutted road. I stop as I always have at the top of the small hill leading down to the level of the cabins and the lake. Our place of safety, where my childhood memories lie heavily in every piece of the place— the happiness of being together with my family, the fun of running around the still waters of the lake, the books I reread every year, the toys that would happily be waiting for me to take them out, the stoic simplicity of it all. Even though it's summer, the weather is mild up here as it has always been, no warmer than the upper seventies, and all the windows in the truck are open. The surface of the water near shore winks through the dense trees that grow as close to the lake as possible, rippling in the afternoon sunlight, sending flashes of silvery-gold water up at us. That view has remained unchanged in my mind since I was a very young boy, and I cherish it. Every. Single. Time.

"It's so pretty," comes Kuniko's soft voice from the bed of the truck.

Yes, yes, it is. It always has been.

The seven of us wearily climb out, unpack all our gear, and let the dogs run free since they'll pick up whether we have any visitors waiting for us. Everyone is sore and tired, but happy.

As Eve gives a welcome tour to our new arrivals, Morgan and I reluctantly go for a quick patrol around the lake in opposing directions, with a dog at our side, meeting at the dense field across the water that's spotted with blueberry bushes—and in one spot, a mammoth-sized blueberry tree that stands proudly at an intersection cut into the waving grass—and other fruit shrubs. No creatures stirring, and for once, Morgan doesn't ask if I want to race back. We simply walk, chatting on the way about nothing and passing the scant houses that sit adjacent to the calm water.

We close in on the second-to-last house a few hundred yards down the shore of the lake before our clutch of dwellings, and Morgan stops for a moment, with something clearly on her mind. I drift to a stop, too, and turn toward her to listen. "Thank you," she says. "I know you didn't want to go, and I know it wasn't the smartest thing to do, but it was the *right* thing to do. Those poor people, even though we only got three of them out, it'll be better for them here. It means a lot to me, like I have some closure."

I nod back and hug her. She's right, of course. It was the right thing to do, and at least we saved a few. It's going to be better for all of us now, and maybe we'll find the ever-elusive tranquility in these mad times. I try to avoid thinking about whether our invasion has cost some of the other innocents their lives, who would otherwise have been spared, though still ensnared by Marcus.

***

We all eat dinner and sit on the front porch in the fleeting light, getting to know each other. One of the things I eventually noticed when Morgan and I would come to visit our grandparents as children was that we always went to bed early, usually no later than nine o'clock, even when we were teens and devoted to staying up as late as possible in case we missed "something." The days had been full of activity, so we were on the move at all times, and then night fell like a cloak dropped from above to swallow the property. That held true even when we had electric light, and it has remained so since our arrival. This suits me fine since I'm more of a morning person anyway, happy enough to rise around five o'clock so I won't miss a drop of the day. Tonight, I can see the fatigue written heavily on each of the faces on the porch, and I know we'll crash perhaps earlier than normal.

Kerosene lanterns hang every few feet from hooks, and while we normally avoid extraneous light, we know we killed all the local zombies, and so we fire up the lanterns to push the shadows away. I look around the group to see how everyone's holding up after such a traumatic event.

Eve sits off to my left and looks drained. She told me how stressed she'd been by her conversations with Marcus, how he'd been so matter of fact about the requirements for residence in his compound. I know she's unsettled by the fight since we managed to keep her out of those before, and finally, I guess that the executions are what unnerved her the most. Both had been well deserved, true, but Eve's personality is such that she could never have pulled the trigger in those circumstances. She's a person who soothes those around her and seeks harmony, compromise, and peace.

Morgan looks tired but more alert than the rest of us, thanks to her seemingly limitless energy. It's like being around a ten-year-old boy who got his hands on too much sugar—she seethes with motion, even when she's still. I doubt she has any regrets for killing Vince. In fact, I'm sure she doesn't. She smiles as she listens to the newcomers tell their stories. That pleases me since her brilliant smile has been in hibernation lately, and it's one that engages everyone nearby, lighting up the room. She's indeed a complicated person; her joys fly beyond those of most, and her infrequent lows are a sulking, morose cavern. Because Morgan always just lives without allowing the conventions and limits of "the rules" to constrain her, she reaches emotional places most of us never do since we won't let ourselves become completely immersed in the moment.

Amy is silent for most of the evening, clearly exhausted. I'm sure the trip had been hard for her, especially since she eavesdropped on the conversation between Eve and Marcus. She, too, had been kept out of the fights over time, hiding with Eve under the floor of the cabin when we'd been invaded by Ned's legion, but she bears a few scratches across her cheeks and forehead now, thanks to our flight. Kids have a less cluttered brain than adults—even if they don't think so—and thus have the ability to literally fall to sleep. I can see her fighting to keep her eyelids open so as not to miss anything, but she's losing the battle. I'll just carry her to bed if needed.

Our new roommates are an intriguing mixture. Kuniko, despite her Japanese name, scarcely looks of Asian descent unless you look closely. There's a hint in the tone of her skin since it's a different kind of pale than Eve, and her eyes lift at their outer corners only a smidge. In fact, if you didn't know her name, you'd be unlikely to guess her ancestry. She speaks softly and often from behind the curtain of straight, silky hair that hangs well down her torso. I suspect that is partly to hide the bruise that mars her prettiness and partly to avoid notice, out of habit from her last "home." She tells us she had been a professional chef in the past and so was in charge of food for the group in Kansas, and is happy to do the same here. Given that we've largely lived off canned food, supplemented by local fresh fruit, we're all happy to see if she can mix things up for us. Even though we saw her shoot Marcus and know there's a measure of cold resolve, I get the impression that out of the three survivors, she's going to need the most cautious handling. Her experiences there seem to still weigh heavily on her; I can see it in her introverted body language and decide I'll do far more listening than talking, as our future unfolds, in order to understand her and help her feel secure.

Bob is the Biker Guy. All of us carry postapocalypse miles, but Bob looks like he might've had some rough times beforehand. I guess he's in his midforties, but his face is lined and deep crows'-feet brace his dark-brown eyes, making him look older. The shaved head may add to the impression, but you can see he has been around the block more than a few times. It turns out he had been the engineer for the group, the one who hooked solar panels up to capture some free energy and ran those to batteries that silently powered smaller appliances, like a coffeepot. I could kiss him except for the part about that being weird. We agree to look at the phone book inside to see if we can find a nearby solar-supply place and arrange some panels on the roof of the main cabin since it's the only one that gets direct sun, even if only for a fairly short time each day. Coffee. Real, brewed coffee! We could have rigged up a generator at any point, but they're loud, which attracts monsters and, honestly, pesters me, too, since this is a place of quiet, so we've eschewed the idea over time. Bob looks in every direction and sees possibilities for improvement, and looks genuinely happy to have a series of tasks in front of him in a new place.

Our final newcomer is Maya. She's as tall as Morgan, athletically built but less muscular than my sister; more like a runner's build. Unlike Kuniko, who is as pale as a sheet, Maya bears a fantastic brown tan that makes her gray-blue eyes even more remarkable. Short, curly brown hair frames her face, though some of it is rebellious and wanders in every direction, which causes her to move a curl or two away fairly often. She's pretty in a tomboyish way, but if you pay attention, you'll notice that if she were to wear makeup and a dress, she would draw all eyes in any room she entered back in the days of makeup and dresses. Her height and carriage emphasize that, as she moves with the same kind of power and confidence Morgan does. Maya had only recently arrived to Marcus's compound. She had been living in California, mostly just surfing and looking for acting gigs, when the zombies appeared and cleared out all the beautiful people. She eventually decided to come east to seek out any surviving family and a change of location. Her stopover had been similar to what happened to Morgan—a pit stop that turned into an overnight invitation that turned into a nightmare trap. She was there for less than a month, but she bears a simmering anger that informs me her rent had been extracted in that time. I decide to tiptoe around her, too, for the time being, but I'm happy we have another physical person with us as long as she gets along with my sibling.

Morgan typically measures herself against everyone, all the time, and an athletic peer is either going to be a good or bad thing, or both. She constantly turns everything into a competition with me, and she's pushed Eve. To her credit,

Eve has pushed back every time, but Morgan needs an equal to keep her out of trouble. Perhaps Maya is going to be the one to fill that role. I'm just going to stay the hell out of the way and let them figure out the pecking order on their own.

All of them are thankful, however, for the rescue and for their new home, and settle in quickly. We're now full to capacity.

***

I still sleep in the main cabin's single bedroom while Morgan, Eve, and Amy are in the second cabin, which has two bedrooms and three beds. Maya and Kuniko take the third building, though we have to haul another bed from one of the other properties down the shore since it's a single bedroom and bath. Bob draws the short straw and sleeps alone in the boathouse, but he has the best morning view out of all of us since he leaves the shuttered doors open to the water and is greeted by the sight of the placid lake each morning.

We busy our days as we had before by gathering water supplies by the truckload from the nearby towns' now-vacant supermarkets, even though we have the spring as backup. Food is similarly collected from everywhere within reach since the group is now so large and Kuniko has some fantastic ideas, and we make sure to empty the shelves of all varieties of dog food and treats for Ajax and Jack. Morgan, Maya, and I patrol the area daily, though as the weeks pass, it feels like it's more for the exercise than for safety since we see nothing at all. Eve and Amy run with us, too, but

Bob takes a pass on that given his injury. Energetic, and occasionally ferocious, games of Wiffle ball ensue across the lake, in the field bordered with a makeshift fence and bare patches for the bases. We're content, safe, and happy, and many an afternoon, we can all be found reading a book from the library we've accumulated over time, on the front porch or in the hammock strung between two looming trees that stand closer to the garage. Despite the gaping hole in the driver's door of the BMW, it still runs happily enough, and I take Amy with me out on drives in the countryside, and eventually (and painfully), I teach her how to drive. It's a stick-shift car, but I agree with my father that everyone should learn to drive stick, even now. We don't worry too much about stop signs or which side of the road to drive on, and I may have let her drive a little faster than the speed limit too.

***

One afternoon, I'm sitting down on the stone wall that keeps the lake contained, drowsily looking at the newts or salamanders—never quite had that figured out—darting under the completely still surface. I've always found looking at water, especially calm water, to be of great solace. Nothing specific is troubling me. I just can't help but wonder, Now what? We saved some more people, we'd killed all the local zombies, we have lots of supplies, and there are now enough of us to feel like we're more of a force to be reckoned with in any future conflict. We're safe, finally, but I'm terrible at being idle and probably need something more to do than just relax here. I'm debating taking a run or a drive, but I'm not debating very hard. My shoes are off, and I dangle my legs in the still, cool water. Even now in the latter stages of summer, the lake is, frankly, damn cold beneath the first foot or so of depth, and my toes teeter on turning into numb little nuggets when I hear a shuffle step behind me, and turn in alarm, and grab for my pistol. Mostly safe or not, guns are always at hand.

It's just Bob awkwardly making his way down the miniature steps that lead down to the bathing area, so I set the gun back down. He sure does a fair zombie imitation with that leg injury of his, and so I finally ask him about that. "That damn Marcus. He knew he needed me for my engineer skills, but he didn't like it that the playing field wasn't level. I could've gone anywhere, I didn't need him, but he needed a guy who could rig stuff up, and so he had that animal Vince hold me down while he cut my Achilles tendon so I couldn't run," he explains angrily.

He turns to show me the back of his left leg, which has a jagged pink scar scrawled across the fat tendon just above the ankle. "It was something he did after Jack escaped and your sister came. He was pissed that she'd been warned about him and didn't stay, and so he started doing this to people, especially ones he didn't want to get away. I can't run, like you saw when we all got away, at least not like I used to be able to. He was going to do it to all of the women, too, but decided it was going to change the way they walked and decided he didn't like that since, in his words, 'a sashay with a limp is not sexy.' The man was sick."

Unreal. If I had any lingering doubts about what we did, this casts those into the faint breeze, blowing them away across the lake. I feel bad for what happened to these people and am once again happy we were able to save (some of) them.

"I'm sorry, man. I know some of what went on there, and to be honest with you, I don't really want to know more details so that I don't dwell on it. I'm hopeful that we're all in a good place now and am glad we were able to help."

He nods and says, "Thanks. Yeah, there was some pretty fucked-up shit going on in there." He sure has that right, and not just about their prison. There has been a bunch of fucked-up shit all over the place. "I was homeless before then, you know," he adds. "I'd had a good job like lots of people, but when the recession blew everything up in 2009, I lost it, then lost my impatient wife and kids, my house, my cars, everything. Went from living in a big house to sleeping under bridges in just over a year. My fault for not saving enough and thinking there wasn't going to be such a thing as a rainy day, though I'm not the only one to make that mistake. The only good thing in that was when all this shit went down, I was already good at hiding so the cops couldn't roust me, so I just stayed under the radar while those monsters wiped the rest of the world out. Marcus's bullshit wasn't anything compared to that, both the being regular homeless and then the zombies making everyone homeless."

I don't really know what to say to all that, so I just nod my head and say, "I hope it's all going to be easier going forward."

***

Time slips by, though we make the most of filling it. We
have fun, but we also have chores. Winter is going to come
again, and the main cabin is the only one with a fireplace,
and even that barely keeps the clutching fingers of winter
in New York at bay. Bob is brilliant at figuring out solutions
to problems, and his skills prove invaluable. He's no office
engineer; his background is in construction since he likes
hands-on work. He'd owned his company but also made it a
point to be out in the field on every job so as to lend a hand,
keep sharp, and keep a pulse on his workers. Solar panels are
installed on every inch of the roof and rigged into running
the baseboard heaters that are needed even on late-summer
mornings. We have coffee, *real* coffee every morning and
anytime we want it. Even though my grandparents would
have cringed, we replace all the ancient single-pane windows
with triple-pane ones for better insulation. Easy enough to
pick them up at the home-improvement stores in the larger
towns nearby and bring them back without having to worry
about inspectors.

The two of us build three-tier bunk beds in the cozy
nook to the right of the front door, along with a ladder for
access to the top two, and a Murphy bed against one of the
family room walls, so we don't lose too much of the already
scant square footage. It had been tight when Top, Amelie,
DeeDee, and I spent our first winter here, so seven people
and two dogs are going to be running into each other. A lot.
Bob draws up plans for an addition off the bedroom and

bath—we intend to tackle in the spring weather—that will be something of a bunkhouse, and we start collecting stones for building chimneys on the three auxiliary cabins in order to add fireplaces at some point, in case our group continues to expand.

"We can stay here forever," Bob says one afternoon as we're sawing raw planks by hand to build a tree house. "All the materials we need are free and abundant. This is an engineer's dream. No budget, no deadline, though being able to use more power tools would help us."

This tree house is one of our escape plans. We still have the panic room under the floor of the cabin, but that will only hold three people in a pinch, and while it's secure, it's also a trap of sorts. Bob's idea is a tree house built up higher on the hill leading away from the lake, one big enough to hold all of us if needed. He puts a ladder against the house, encases the chimney in scaffolding we can climb, with a platform at the top. Off that, he's rigged up a ropes course, one rope low to walk on, two up above waist height to hold. That connects to a tree up the hill where he's added another platform for the transition to more ropes, more platforms, and finally to a clutch of close-growing hemlocks that are going to be the foundation of the tree house. This way, if we need to escape suddenly, we can scramble onto the roof, pull the ladder up behind us, follow the circuit of the ropes to the tree house while being safely twenty feet off the ground, and then swing down to the ground from the tree house more than 250 yards from the cabin. The hillside is virtually impossible to scale on foot, so anyone pursuing us will have to use both hands and feet to chase, and their progress will be slow.

I come up with the idea of a few lookout and hiding spots scattered around the property, where we build more small platforms up in the trees and camouflage them from sight. An extra hammock is used to create an even more clever arrangement in the garage. We sling it tightly from two of the high beams so it doesn't hang down into view through the open door, but anyone inside the hammock will have a clear view of the driveway while remaining unseen.

Maya and Morgan are largely in charge of patrols while we make vast piles of sawdust. Each of them takes a dog with them and goes off for hours at a time in whatever direction they choose, sweeping for whatever may threaten our peace. They arrive back in the early afternoon for lunch, jump in the lake to clean up and cool off, eat, and then work on hand-to-hand skills. It looks like an exercise class in the park with Morgan leading the three other women in drills with their bare hands, the Bo—she asked Bob to make three more, which he did happily after some trial and error with what wood type should be used: oak—and then strength training. The ladies do burpees, planks, push-ups (the "dude" kind), and anything else my sister dreams up. Then more bathing.

At first, Kuniko and Maya are extremely self-conscious when taking a bath in the lake, insisting Bob and I be out of sight. No doubt this is due to their recent experiences, but after a few weeks, they become comfortable enough that the two of us men pose no threat, and they don't mind if we're around. Kuniko remains modest, however, and wears shorts and a few layers of T-shirts at all times. Maya is less concerned and wears a purple bathing suit, finally laughing and loosening up to explain that everyone in California had been in a race to wear the least clothes on the beach anyway, so her normal-shaped bikini that "actually covers her ass" is practically nun like. She has a radiant smile that erupts from her tanned face like a time-lapse photo series of a flower opening. Her figure is lovely, trim with rippling muscles emerging everywhere, the benefit of the myriad exercise fads on the West Coast, not to mention the whole living-on-the-run-for-years thing followed by the physical torture imposed by my sister. Maya's attractive, no doubt, and my age, too, but in a way, she's no different from my sister in my eyes, and I view her as just like a sibling.

I still only have eyes for Eve. The ridiculous voice inside my head insists I should only have *hands* for Eve, or that I should move on, but that isn't how I work. Even back before all of this, I never initiated something with a woman but would wait until she decided. I've probably sent a lot of mixed messages to girls over the years as a result, but it makes sense to me that if the girl starts the kissing and such, it means she's sure about it and me. Unfortunately for my eyes—and for another part of me—Eve still wears the infamous yellow bikini that had driven Ned to madness and betrayal. Yeah, the one that's a bit see-through up top and forces me to tear my eyes away anytime we all happen to be down at the water at the same time. Maya and Morgan both wear athletic-type swimsuits—yes, they're bikinis, too, but with full coverage on the caboose and more of a sports-bra cut up top. Eve's suit is worthy of a salute since it's cut high on the hips, barely covers her compact breasts, and is pretty damn transparent.

Um, you already mentioned that. Though, I can see why you might go back to it. Why are you distracting me, anyway? I'm focused on the view.

I take it as something of a compliment that she feels comfortable enough to still wear it after what happened with Ned. He had become fascinated with her after spending winter with her (and Amy) in their Pennsylvania shelter, but there was no reciprocity. After they came here, he went out one afternoon for parts to repair my grandfather's BMW. When he came back, he saw me watching Eve bathe in that very swimsuit and accused her of being an attention whore before storming off. Shortly after that, he obviously decided that if he couldn't be with her, all of us deserved to die, and so he drove down to the town, lured the zombies back, and tried to set them loose on us. It all backfired on him, though, when Morgan pinned him to the door of the car with a crossbow bolt, and the monsters attacked him before coming after the rest of us. We were able to secure Amy and Eve in the panic room while Morgan and I led the horde on a chase around the lake, picking some of them off as we ran and then wiping the rest out in a final battle.

There have been no slumber parties since Eve arrived; her habit of coming into my room to sleep next to me (though facing away) had ended in North Carolina. That may have had something to do with DeeDee and I getting together briefly before she was killed by a swarm of yellowjackets, the Ned thing, or just the curious way things work in the minds of women. No matter, I'm still mesmerized by her. She's a lot like me—quiet and introverted for the most part and content with silence. Where we differ is in our reactions to threats; she's mostly a peacekeeper and even kept me from killing Jack—not the pirate nor the dog—oh so long ago. She's the same here. She moves through all of us, providing a calming presence whenever anyone is out of sorts—like Morgan or one of Morgan's victims—and a soothing presence who rests a hand on an arm when it's needed. She quietly assists with all tasks whether it be cooking or gathering firewood. Eve sets the mood for the group, though I doubt she's aware she does so; it's just her way. I satisfy myself with watching her as I have always done. Sometimes, it's enough to just watch *that* person. Not in a lustful way, but more in a yearning way. Having her in sight makes me happy and content.

In short, life is good, or as good as it can be. Like always, it's never quite that simple.

CHAPTER 12

Summer is winding down, and the mornings are beginning to get even cooler. Even though it's rarely humid here, the air is drying out and bears a crisp harbinger of the forthcoming serious weather. Shorts and short sleeves are rarer now; only in the middle of the day or when across the lake—which is curiously much warmer than our side—and bathing becomes something we get out of the way quickly rather than lingering. All of us are down at the shoreline, and most everyone is in the water. I'm just skipping rocks and thinking about grabbing one of the stray golf clubs from a barrel in the garage and some range balls to hit like I saw my uncle do once. It's a pleasant, clear afternoon, and we're taking full advantage of it. We ate lunch outside and took a stroll around the path encircling the lake earlier, and aside from the happy sounds from the bathing area, it's quiet as usual.

Until I hear a humming sound. Not a hummingbird hum, a mechanical one.

Both of the dogs perk their ears at the same time, scanning the sky for the source of the noise like I'm doing. A fleck appears in the sky from the far side of the lake, looking no larger than a vulture or hawk, but it grows as it approaches us. Everyone hears it now and clambers toward the stone wall, wrapping towels around them and standing to watch.

It's a drone. Not one of the little toy drones that started to become popular for the general public back in the day. This is a big one, nearly six feet in diameter, painted black and with propellers whirring on each corner that pivot independently as the machine settles into a hover above the surface of the water a couple of dozen yards away from us. It has a camera under the body; I can see the reflection of the lens on the face of a baseball-sized bulge under the carriage, and it pans from side to side to bring us all into view. How bizarre. A drone. Aircraft vanished as quickly as everything else when the world had come to an abrupt, screaming, painful end, but here's some sign of technology and, well, other people.

Everyone begins talking at once.

"What does it mean?"

"Who could it be?"

"Should we be nervous?"

Bob watches it closely as the camera captures us, then shifts direction and goes back the way it had come. "That's military," he says. "I'm sure of it. Some of the magazines I got back in the day showed prototypes of ones just like it, but it wasn't for retail sale. It's a military bird for sure."

The only thing that remains to be seen is whether it's a good thing or a bad one. I think about Top. He once said the military has a survival plan for everything, even something like a zombie apocalypse. As outlandish an idea as that sounded, I'm wondering now if he had been on to something.

***

Another week passes without anything notable happening. We're in a heightened state of awareness, not so much alert since there hadn't been anything overtly ominous about the flying gadget. But someone has come looking for, and at, us. So we keep our eyes peeled, stick a little closer to home, and ensure no one patrols or goes out for supplies alone. I find myself looking skyward throughout the day but see nothing. If the new world has taught us anything, it's that you take the days and challenges as they arrive but remain prepared for anything to change on short notice. The group takes loaded weapons to bed anyway, but now, we all move them even a little closer to the bed and talk about having everyone sleep in the main cabin as we will in the winter, but then we decide it isn't necessary.

Tonight, Ajax sleeps at the foot of my bed, and Jack is with the girls in cabin number two since he's completely fixated on Morgan and almost never lets her out of his sight. I think it'll be nice to find two more dogs so we can have an alarm system in each cabin.

Ajax wakes me from a deep sleep later that evening. The utter darkness of our little settlement combined with busy, physical days makes for good rest each night, especially since we're clear of the monsters loitering in town. Ajax doesn't bark, he's too smart for that, but rather gets up from his bed of quilts on the floor and comes to nudge a wet nose against my hand that dangles over the edge of the bed, with a faint whisper of a growl that seems impossibly subtle for a hundred-pound Rottweiler.

I'm awake, fully awake, immediately. I listen with every bit of focus I have for a full minute but pick up nothing. It's completely dark outside, without even a hint of the sun rising over the hillside behind us. My heart rate takes off while I hold utterly still and scan the window overlooking the porch for motion, and see nothing. Ajax appears to be up and alert for a reason, so I settle my bare feet on the floor, taking care to settle my weight gradually to avoid any squeaks of century-old wood. I shrug a sweatshirt on over my head and let my fingers drift to the .45 on the bedside table.

Safety off. Good.

I pause and bend down to slide socks onto my feet so that instead of taking full steps, I can slip my feet along the floor to the windows without making a sound. Nothing visible outside, so I go into the main room, careful to skirt the edges of the rug and hug the walls. I sense Ajax following me. If a dog can tiptoe, he's doing so since I can't hear even a stray click of nails on the floor. Crouching down before reaching the larger span of windows, I stop again and wish the windows were open so I can hear too. I try to settle my breathing and heartbeat since it's hammering in my ears, and I hold my position for several minutes, looking for motion outside.

Nada, zero, zip.

The moon had long dropped beyond the western horizon, and I may as well be blindfolded in a cave for all I'm able to see. It's time to go outside, and I'm torn between going out the front door or making my way back and through the kitchen to the rear. I decide to do the latter. The porch is definitely squeaky, while the back door opens onto the pavers that make up the paths between cabins, so I'll be silent on those. I slide my way through the dining area, still watching the windows and seeing nothing, cruise across the kitchen's linoleum floors, and ease the heavy back door open inches at a time. The smell of the outdoors creeps in, along with a faint breeze, and I push slowly against the screen door that opens outward, being conscious of the spring that will bang it closed, to the never-ending chagrin of my grandmother. We make it outdoors in the ebony-cloaked world, and just as Ajax pushes my hand once more with his rough snout, I feel something cool and hard press against my neck. I freeze, and the dog growls deep in his chest.

"I know the dog doesn't understand English, but if either one of you moves a hair, you're gonna have a shitty start to your day. Get him to stand down, sir, however you need to do it." A calm, commanding voice comes from just over my left shoulder. He must have been against the wall of the building, just waiting for me to exit. Dammit.

I ease my hand over to find Ajax's head and pat him, roughing my hand across his pumpkin-sized head in what I hope is a don't-bark-your-ass-off-and-chase-after-whoever-just-spoke kind of way.

"I can see your gun, sir. Do not move. I am going to relieve you of your weapon. Finger off the trigger, slow and easy, that's right. Hold the barrel with finger and thumb." The ghost in the darkness pulls the .45 from my fingers, though I still can't see a fucking thing. "Okay, we're good. All clear at the rear of cabin Alpha. Man one and dog R under supervision."

I feel Ajax sit beside me and keep my hand steady on him. My thoughts are spinning, though clearly, this is a military thing, and if they were hostile, I'd already be dead, so I keep still and my mouth shut. I'll just wait and see what's going on, though I worry briefly about the others.

"Sir, we are going to move forward to the space between this cabin and the garage building. I have night-vision goggles on and can see you as clearly as if you were a snowflake on a black blanket, so no sudden moves or foolishness with the dog. The dog is covered, too, by my squad, so you are to cooperate and follow instructions," he continues. "Alpha One moving to rendezvous position. We are clear here."

The path to where he wants me to go isn't more than a dozen steps, and I flirt with the idea of darting around the corner. But obviously, he has company, and I'll probably run right into more trouble, so I discard the idea quickly. I know the steps by heart, even in the dark—Morgan and I would sneak out of the window in the second cabin when we were kids, to creep around at night, not for anything specific but just because she thought it'd be fun, just like it was on our street at home.

Morgan.

Shit.

A sudden racket sounds from the far side of the main cabin, back toward the cabin where she sleeps with Eve and Amy. Cursing, *lots* of cursing from both a male and female, and the sound of a struggle. I hear Jack suddenly go batshit, baying his head off in a deep snarl of warning, and Ajax tightens up at my hip with a heavy growl bubbling out of his barrel chest.

"Sir, I repeat, hold your position and do not move. You will receive no additional warning."

Suddenly, dozens of floodlights click on, blinding me. It reminds me of being caught outside the walls in Kansas City, and I tense reflexively. They cover the entire area with harsh, clean illumination as though the sun has just popped spontaneously into view. My guard has raised his goggles and now wears opaque sunglasses against the glare. Yep, army guy, all dressed in camo, helmeted, and with gear hanging from all over his uniform. He's got a short-barreled automatic weapon pointed steadily at my chest from ten steps away. There's a second guy behind him, with his gun lined up on Ajax, and then even more of them emerge from the shadows behind the garage. Two come off the porch, and three more appear from an inflatable boat tied to one of the birch trees along the shore. It's an invasion.

The noise, predictably, is due to my sister. As we come around to the front of the house, I turn to look across the porch and see her facing off with a soldier. All she's wearing is a huge T-shirt of mine, and her bare legs shine in the false morning light. Eve and Amy are already secured by a couple of other men, and I see Bob, Kuniko, and Maya in a similar situation though not held, just guarded. Morgan, however, isn't going to go peacefully, nor is Jack, who refuses to leave her side. Morgan holds her Bo at the ready, and the soldier is weaponless. His rifle lays on the ground off to the side, but like any good trooper, he isn't going to let that stop him. He holds his gloved hands out in front of him, looking for an opening to subdue her. Again, I remind myself that if they'd come with really bad intent, we'd already be dead, and I can tell he's trying not to hurt her.

I also know he's about ten seconds away from getting his ass firmly kicked since she has no such compunction.

Just as I see her raise the Bo, I hear a "Ten hut!" and jerk around to see a single man stroll through the crowd. No helmet, no heavy gear or rifle, just a dark-green beret on his head and pistol in a holster at his hip. "I think that's about enough of that. Drop the staff, ma'am. *Now.* I'm not in the business of having my boys beat up on women but will let Sergeant Williams do so if you don't comply right this instant." He speaks in a gruff voice that's used to commanding and shows he's accustomed to obedience. What he doesn't know is that he's picked the wrong girl to try and boss around.

"Sergeant Williams is welcome to try his luck!" she shouts back. "I hope you boys brought your first aid kits and a stretcher because he's going to have a permanent limp. I'm not dropping anything except soldier-boy to the ground!"

"Okay then, your decision. Lessons get learned the hard way sometimes. Go ahead, Cody. Secure your target but try not to hurt her too much."

As I watch the commander, I see he has an eagle pinned to his uniform. I think this means "colonel," which also means "big dog."

As I predicted, Morgan beats the shit out of the poor kid. He drops his helmet and shrugs out of his backpack but has no other nonlethal weapon at hand, and she takes advantage of that quickly. One, two hard and blindingly fast thwacks to his knee and opposite ankle, and Cody is hobbling around unsteadily, unsure of which injury to favor. He rushes at her, trying to use his weight and strength as an asset, but she gracefully dances to the side and spins the Bo around in a wicked circuit as he passes harmlessly by. She then cracks him across the shoulders, sending him tumbling face-first into the turf. He doesn't move, and I'm unsure if he's either injured, mortified, or maybe just unconscious. I know she could've crippled him if she wanted to by aiming higher at the back of his skull, but my sister isn't trying to kill anyone either; she's just resisting being told what to do for only about the millionth time in her life.

"Anyone else?" she snarls, standing proudly over his prone body, Bo wrapped behind her.

Several of the soldiers make as if to move in, but the commander makes a disgusted snort and calls his boys off. "Ma'am, you've made your point, and well. I can see that *Corporal* Williams is going to have to spend more time in his hand-to-hand combat courses. Someone help him up and get him a bandage for his ego."

A pair of the other soldiers move over to pick up the dazed fellow, who shrugs off their helping hands as he makes it to his feet and glares at Morgan. I'm sure he isn't going to hear the end of this from his peers for quite some time, but he isn't the first, or last, to seriously underestimate her.

"Now, where were we? Is there a leader of this little group handy?"

Everyone looks over at me, and I step forward. "We, that is, all of us were quietly sleeping, in case you hadn't noticed."

"Son, anyone who's read their military history knows that the best time to surprise people is the really wee hours of the day. That's why we came when we did, though to their credit, your dogs did their job, so I tip my hat to them," he replies with a nod toward Jack, who's still bristling over at Morgan's feet.

"Why are you here? What do you want? Aside from that little, um, show, it's obvious you're not here to hurt us, or you would have come in differently. We're not bothering anyone here." I'm angry, partly at the interruption of our peace and partly because it seems like if the military is still around, we could have used their help over the past couple of years with those, oh, you know, hordes of *fucking zombies* all over the world.

He looks directly at me for a moment, then shifts his stance, relaxing somewhat. "Why don't we all stand down? Boys, weapons at rest. Squads out to the perimeter, on guard, but we're going to need some coffee, posthaste."

"I'll make the coffee," pipes up Kuniko.

He smiles at her and nods, and she slips indoors, followed by Amy.

***

The seven of us settle on the porch after Kuniko brews a pot of morning happiness. Everyone's a bit disheveled after the abrupt wake-up call. Morgan went back into her cabin and came back with some shorts on; I did the same since a sweatshirt and boxers are what I'd come outside in. All the soldiers dispersed from the immediate area, and a Humvee trundled heavily down the driveway while the coffee was being prepared. I don't know how many people make up a squad or battalion or whatever, but this is a sizeable group. At least twenty scatter in each direction down the path, a few stand watchfully at the top of the driveway on the flat space we used for a basketball court, so a lot of firepower is concentrated in our space. I look longingly at their automatic rifles before they fade into the shadows of the early morning and tree cover, thinking about how handy a few of those would've been over the years.

The colonel, since that's what he is now that we've gotten through introductions, sips his coffee, smiles, and raises his cup to Kuniko. "That's a fine brew, ma'am. Real coffee. Thank you. The army is good at a lot of things, and strong coffee is one of them. However, coffee that actually *tastes* like coffee is not. I apologize for the method of your wakeup, but we knew you were armed and thought marching down the driveway and from other directions might spark a fight, and that is not our intent. Better to come in quiet, secure the area, and talk civilly."

He looks over at Morgan and nods. "My boys are superb troops, and you made Cody look bad in front of his squad mates. Good for you. It's a lesson for him to take any threat seriously. I'd like to think he was holding back, and I bet he'd like to think the same, but I could use a few more like you with that edge."

"Sir, not to cut in, but why are you here?" I'm impatient to find out the point of all this, why they've come, and what he has in mind.

He gazes at me thoughtfully for a moment. "Son," he begins, "I hope you don't mind me calling you that."

I shake my head. It reminds me of Top, who did the same, and I feel an ache over his absence. My guess is when you're in the military and in doubt for names, you just call everyone "son."

"We're checking out any groups of more than a couple," the colonel continues, "just seeing who survived, what they're doing, and what they're up to. I have patrols all over this area of the state right now. We use satellites and infrared to locate groups, send the drones in to take a look, and then come to inspect and offer a choice."

"A choice of what?" I ask. "We're fine here. We got all of the local zombies not too long ago. We're just trying to live quietly and safely."

"That's just it. We're offering sanctuary in settlements with others. We have a half dozen of those around the country so far. The world has to be rebuilt, and we're bringing survivors together so we can get around to the business of doing that. The people who've made it this far are the toughest of the tough, and we need all of those kinds of folks to start over."

"Wait, you said you still have satellites, and we saw the drone. And you have camps all over. Are you telling me that the military has been up and running this whole time?" I feel my anger rising a bit, and I'm bothered by his use of the word "sanctuary" given our recent history.

"We are five by five and have been all this time, though there's fewer of us than originally planned. Supplies, walls, farms, aircraft, tanks. You name it, we've got it. Big, sprawling compounds where survivors can live freely. We've got miles of barbed wire to keep any wandering critters out, lookout towers. We have it all." He sits back in the rocking chair, sips at his coffee again, and looks rather pleased with himself for his offer.

I think about what he just said, about living free but behind walls and barbed wire. It sounds more like the place we'd just invaded than the one we have here, and I assume there will be rules and regimens there too. "Originally planned? Not sure I follow you there."

He makes a face, not a guilty one, but an expression of "whoops, didn't mean to say that." He looks around our group, one at a time, and then takes a deep breath. "There is no way to sugarcoat this, so I'll give it to you straight. This, all of this," he says with a wave in all directions, "is no accident."

Bob is the first to speak from among our stunned group. "The fuck you mean this isn't an accident? D'you mean someone on our side created those things and then let it all happen?" I can hear the fury in his voice and admit I'm feeling the same way.

The colonel sighs. "It's something of a long story, but since none of you can post this to Facebook or whatever, I'll tell you the highlights. The years since 9/11 have been a time of change in our country and the whole world. The bad guys had a face now, we made sure to show it to Americans often, trying to keep everyone on alert and working together to make it a better world. You remember back when it happened? Everyone was on the same side, here in the US anyway. Democrats, Republicans, splinter groups, all of them holding hands and playing nice, clapping for the president when he addressed the nation, looking for ways to help the families of the first responders to all the sites, and the families of the victims. Everyone in the same boat for a change. For, like, five minutes. We could've been fine. Hell, we could've been great. People were thinking about moving the country in a single direction, together, less political bullshit, more folks helping each other. But then, far too soon, it went right back to the way it'd been. Dems want this,'Pubs want that, and they're like goddamn kids fighting over a rusty toy car in a sandbox. It's a piece of shit, pardon my language, ladies, but it's the only prize, so they fight to keep it away from the other. It's not about wanting it. It's about wanting the other side to not get what they want."

He stops for a swig of coffee but makes a face. It must have gone cold while he was talking. "Jesus," he says. "Hot coffee is the motor that gets the world going. Iced coffee is wonderful, too, on a summer day. But room-temperature coffee is disgusting. Anyway, the handcuffs were on the military too. 'Go to Afghanistan,' they said, 'find the bad guys, but do it nicely and shoot second, not first.' That country is impossible to take without our big weapons. Not smart missiles, not patrols, not helicopters. Those aren't enough. Look at what happened to Russia when they tried. They don't even play by the rules, and they got nowhere. How were we supposed to do better with our hands tied? No, the only way to take that country is to nuke it back to the Stone Age and let whoever's god sort it out after, but no one was going to give us the go-ahead to use even tactical nukes. Not in this day and age. All of the moaning and groaning for the poor innocents that got wiped out, too, would've been too much. Though 'innocent,'" he says with actual air quotes, "is a bullshit word in that part of the world. Look how many times we've been enemies with a country, then back pumping money and weapons into them two years later so we can get oil, and then back round and round. Not just the Middle East either. North Korea was getting up to more trouble than the public was aware, Russia was getting back to some of their own bad habits, and China was the elephant in the room that was just waiting for the right time to flex their muscles."

I want to say something or ask a question, but I simply open my mouth and shut it again since I can't come up with anything.

"All of those countries," he continues, "plus a bunch of enemies in others, hated us. America was the wealthiest and most powerful empire in the history of the modern world. We had the best of everything, or so they thought, and just like our politicians with each other, they wanted us not to have it. Not to fix their own country by learning from us. No, sir. By ruining it, or taking it away. Anyone who didn't see this kind of behavior infesting the world was blind as could be. People wanted to tear things down, tear others down rather than build, create, and improve like we'd done in the past. Even our own were reaching their hands out to the government saying, 'Give me this and that,' and then complained that the free help wasn't enough. Heaven forbid, people got sweaty, got their hands dirty, or used their brains. I know you all saw that. Maybe you just didn't think about it the same way we did in the services. A small group of us, some from each branch, started thinking and talking. Soldiers are historians. We learn from the mistakes of the past, like don't invade Russia in winter, or really, ever. Too darn big, and their leaders don't bat an eye at thousands of corpses. They see them as a useful barricade and fewer mouths to feed. Our cadre came to the realization that it was time to start over in a more, let's say, comprehensive way. This was no easy decision, mind you. But there were too many threats from too many directions, and we were too hamstrung to really take care of business the right way, one bad-guy group at a time, and we couldn't do it in a traditional way. Once we all got onto the same page and saw the only course of action we could take, we started planning. The brightest minds in the services, working together, ran thousands of scenarios for what to do. Did we break from the government and finally do things without restraint? We have enough bombs to start at the corner of an enemy country and turn it to smoking rubble inch by inch up to the far corners. Give that one a try? 'Don't think about civilians, think about logistics,' we told our planners. Chemical weapons. We've got those too. Nukes, big ones and little ones, and everything in between. We have all of the goods, just not permission to use them. That pointed to our problem being bigger than the outside world. Some of it was here at home, as hard as that message is to hear. We'd never acquire that approval to engage without restraint. And even if we had, heaven forbid, we would piss off the indignant internet and antisocial media with pictures of dead kids and blown-up apartment buildings and so on. After a lot of discussion and modeling the outcomes, we had to discard most of the options and were down to one viable alternative. It had a bunch of different names. 'Operation Reset' was the most popular, but there were others too. My preference was 'Roll the Bones' since that's what we were doing. The pathogen was airborne, you see, with a ninety-eight percent mortality rate, a one-point-nine-nine percent conversion rate, and then there's you people. The point-one percent survival rate. Of course, the two percent took care of a shitload more of the survivors, too, maybe more than we expected, but we were committed to letting things fall where they did once it was kicked off. Our best estimate is that there are now fewer than a half-million people left on the entire planet, maybe a good bit less than that."

He stops talking, finally, maybe to let it all sink in.

I'm stunned. Our own government, or at least a subset of it, had intentionally ended the world as we knew it. Including our own people. Including every-freaking-body's people. Hundreds of millions dead. Billions dead. Millions of zombies. A few hundred thousand remnants. I don't know what to say, or think. The numbers are too big to grasp in any kind of context, like an old quote from mid-twentieth century, something about a single death is a tragedy, but millions is a statistic. The rest of my group is similarly speechless, and I see tears in all their eyes and find the same in my own. I didn't even realize it.

"For … for all the crappy stuff," I start, not being able to find adequate words. "For as bad as things seemed to be, you decided to just *end* it all without giving people a second chance. All of it—"

"Look, son, I know this is unpleasant to hear. We feel bad about what had to happen. But at the same time, it's a chance for those of us left to get it right going forward. No more nonsense about oil, conflicting political agendas, media run amok, entitled people, the selfishness that was beginning to pervade our lazy countrymen, finger-pointing, or our leaders forgetting how to lead versus collecting power to themselves. 'All of it' is right. We brought all of that to a stop all at once. I don't expect that you'd agree with the method since nonmilitary types might not view this in the same perspective, but we're confident in the outcome."

"What about the alpha zombies? How did you cook those up?" I'm curious just how far their experiments went.

"Is that what you call them? That's a good name. Well, those ones we haven't exactly figured out. We didn't create a second strain of the disease, so we just chalked them up to dumb luck." His eyes dart sideways as he says all this, and I suspect there's more to the story than he's letting on, but I can't exactly interrogate him. "There aren't too many of them, though, so we're not considering them a viable threat at this point in time."

Oh, so the smart ones who control and direct the mindless ones? There's nothing to worry about regarding those. No, not at all. He's so matter of fact. Just saying this is "unpleasant to hear," and they're "confident in the outcome." Just dispensing with the whole we-just-executed-billions-of-humans part of it. I'm appalled, even if some of what he said for why they'd done it makes a certain amount of logical sense. Some of what Marcus had been selling made sense, too, but that doesn't make it right. My god, it really is all just statistics to him—figure out how best to kill most of the planet and then hit the "Go" button.

"You can see the problems we've solved," he continues to explain, to my annoyance. "No more threat from any of the countries that despised us. We, uh, ran some cleanup operations after dispersal in a number of those just to make sure we got to full ratios. Food shortages? Done. Global warming, if that was a thing caused by people and their machines and cities? Solved. Oil prices or availability? No longer an issue. Pirates on the eastern coast of Africa? Fish food. Texting and driving? Adios cellphones, Wi-Fi, and driving itself, for the most part. Media out of control? Now, they're eating each other instead. You name the woe, it's been wrapped up in a bow, albeit a messy one for a while there. We sorted out nearly every issue facing the world. Every empire comes to an end when it collapses under the weight of its excess, and it was time for someone to be brave enough to provide the push."

Bob stands at this point, his chair jerking backward from his legs as he does so, and stares at the colonel as if about to say something, but then he just shakes his head sadly and walks away without a word. Amy trails behind him, catching up and taking his hand as they head over to the parking area away from all of us. Morgan is the only one to say anything, which is an all-too-clear mumble: "Assholes." That's a good word but not strong enough. I think about DeeDee's mantra, which was that everyone deserves a second chance no matter how badly they fucked up their first. Our own people had removed that as an option, for everyone; hell, they even took away most humans' chance to even mess up the first time. All of it is mind-bending, and even though it finally gives us an answer to what happened after years of fighting to survive, the scale of it and callous disregard for life is an unfair trade for that sad piece of knowledge.

The colonel interrupts my thoughts. "So, you all have an opportunity here. We can offer you safety, the company of a much larger group, the comfort of easy food and water, really anything you could want. The exchange is simple. We're going to rebuild America, the right way, and we can use people like all of you, who have shown the grit to survive. Look at all of you. Fit, tough, ingenious, survivors. You're the kind of people we need and want. I have helicopters at my disposal a few minutes away. All you'd have to do is pack whatever you need, and we're off. You can even bring the dogs, though I'm not sure how they'll handle a chopper ride." He gets quickly to his feet. "We'll step away and give you some time to decide. We'll rendezvous in one hour." He calls his troops to muster, and they all make their way over to the driveway. After the colonel gets into the Humvee with a few others, they head up and away.

I know what my answer is, but it isn't just about me. The idea of leaving here is bad enough since I've been fond of this place for decades and will happily remain. Trusting our new "friend" will be impossible. Someone who represents a group of strangers who'd pulled the plug on almost the entire world's population? Hell no. Besides, his camps sound like bigger versions of what we just destroyed. Just a bigger prison where someone else makes the rules. If things don't go right in their idea of what the new America is supposed to look like, what's to stop them from issuing another mass-execution order? I'm going to take my chances out here, thank you very much.

Bob and Amy meander back to the porch now that the soldiers have left, and the seven of us sit around in silence, everyone processing what we just heard. More coffee seems like a grand idea, though whiskey, and a lot of it, seems more appropriate despite the early hour. As if reading my mind, Kuniko ducks into the kitchen and brings more coffee out, pouring it in the group's outstretched mugs before sitting back down.

"All of our decisions have been group ones so far," I say. "But this time, it's different. This decision is for everyone to make on their own and for the rest of the group to respect." I scan the faces around me, from the familiar ones to our new arrivals. "I'm going to stay, and I'll decide for Ajax too. He's staying."

One by one, everyone else takes their turn to call out their decision. Morgan goes first, angrily muttering something along the lines of, "Like this is a question. I'm staying." Clearly, she still wants to fight everyone who just left. Eve and Amy follow, saying they, too, are staying, as does Bob. I'm curious about our other newcomers since they've been somewhere larger and secured by walls and had, from a monsters-only perspective, been safe. So, the offer on the table may possibly be appealing to them.

Maya says she's happy here and would like to stay if we'll have her. The rest of us nod, of course. Someone has to go last, and that's Kuniko. For the first time since I've met her, she sweeps her hair fully away from her face and snaps it into a quick ponytail before speaking. She's a pretty woman; the bruise faded from her cheek some weeks ago, but she still seems like she's trying to fade into the background and avoid notice. I wonder if that's due solely to her recent mistreatment, or if she's been that way her whole life. Some women are uncomfortable with being attractive on the outside if they don't feel settled on the inside.

"I want to stay, too, please," she says. "We haven't been here for a long time, but I love it. It's simple, safe enough, beautiful, and quiet here, and that feels right to me. I know we're at risk maybe a bit more, living out in the open like this, but the alternative of being behind walls and men with guns again isn't living, in my opinion. We'd be waiting, and that's all we were doing in Kansas City. Waiting for the monsters to come, waiting to kill them when they did, waiting for a summons from Marcus for tribute, just *waiting* as the days ticked by. I want to live life the right way and take it as it comes, every moment. He called his place a sanctuary, which was unfair. That's a word I've always liked. It implies somewhere comfortable, cozy, and where you can let the bad things go. *This* is what sanctuary is supposed to feel like. I'm happy here, happier than I've ever been in my life. I'm staying too." She stands up and looks at all of us. "Let's go tell them. We don't have to wait for them to come back. I don't want them to come back here either. It feels like they're tainted."

The colonel had given us an hour, and our decision took less than ten minutes. "Is everyone sure?" I ask. "We don't know how they're going to react, but we can't fight them. It's one thing to be outnumbered by zombies with only enough brains to eat, but another thing with trained soldiers. This means you, too, Morgan."

She smiles over at me and stands up. When she then reaches for her Bo, she pauses briefly before pulling her hand back. "You're right," she says. "We go without weapons, and we tell them. I bet they're at the top of the driveway, out on the main road. Whatever happens, happens, like Kuniko was saying."

The seven of us and the dogs march up the driveway and make for the road. It would make for a nice movie visual. The driveway is a hardscrabble course that winds through the woods, with thin light filtering through the birches to illuminate little pockets on the ground where ferns grew in leafy abundance. We walk up the first, then second hill and begin the trek down the gentle decline toward where we can eventually see the Humvee parked across the entrance to the driveway. Men in uniform emerge silently from cover as we approach, escorting us the final hundred yards or so, and we all stop at once near the nose of the truck. The colonel gets out and says, "Well, that was quick. Where's your gear?"

"We're not coming with you," I reply. "Thanks for your offer, but we've decided to take our chances here, simple as that."

"All of you? Even the feisty one?" he asks, sounding disappointed and looking over at my sister. "I could use someone like you back at the camp. Teach folks there a bit of attitude. You?" he asks, looking at Bob this time. "The engineer? You'd be really helpful too."

They both shake their heads. We're staying. Now, it's a question of how he'll react. I'm surprised at his next words.

"Folks, I can't say I think you're making the right decision, at least, not in my book. We're armed to the teeth at the camps, we have supplies for years and years, and we have a secure perimeter. You wouldn't have to worry about anything, just pitch in and help us all get restarted. But, while most people have decided to join us, some haven't, and we respect that decision. We recognize that unwilling people aren't going to add anything to us and might cause turmoil, and we don't want that either. Here, take this." He holds out a cellphone-like thing to me. "Call me if you change your mind."

I shake my head again. "No, thanks. We'll do this on our own."

He drops his hand, shrugs, and climbs back into the Humvee, which quickly turns around and heads down the dirt road toward the paved one, trailing a sullen-looking, dusty cloud behind him. The rest of his troops form up, nod at us, and jog off into the distance.

It's over.

CHAPTER 13

We take our time walking back to the cabins and the lake, speaking little on the way. I feel relief now that they're gone and have allowed us to stay here, that we rescued Kuniko, Bob, and Maya, that we killed another big squad of zombies, and in a small way, that we know the truth, or more of it anyway. It's an ugly truth, but sometimes, they are.

Normally, Morgan would issue her challenges verbally, but this time, she just takes off down the driveway at full speed, glancing over her shoulder to see how many of us pursue her. Only Maya and I take the bait, and we race pell-mell back in the direction of the cabins, pushing each other playfully and laughing as we run, wordlessly settling into a crisp jog that brings us home all at the same time.

There isn't much else for us to do now except continue like we have been: building, gathering, taking time to smell the roses and pick the blueberries—especially when it means more for the mouth than for the cup—and living in a simple place without the noise of the old, or new world, for that matter. I'm okay with that, and over the course of the next few weeks, I can see the others feel the same way. All of them are content and relaxed, and that makes me happy.

I've always liked movies where, after the film finishes and credits are rolling, they pop little paragraphs onto the screen about what happens next for the main characters. Nothing significant usually, but a little teaser that lets you carry the story forward in your mind, like "so-and-so from a hardscrabble background gets married and has a child who grows up to be president," or "this guy goes on to star for a pro baseball team," and so on. Stories always end when our storytellers decide they're finished, and it's up to us to figure out the rest of it inside our minds. I'm hoping for something simple for us, like "everyone lived happily ever after," but I'm satisfied with "everyone lived," for now.

We're a weird little group with diverse personalities, but it's going to work for us. We're safe, supplied with everything we need, unconstrained by walls or rules or despots, and happy. I feel less necessary than I had been before; there are fewer problems to solve and less zombies to kill (none, actually), and I'm glad to skip being on alert around the clock.

**

Some weeks later, as the summer weather starts to wane in earnest, we get near the point where we'll have to close the windows and doors at bedtime, but I'm being stubborn about that. I love hearing the sounds of the night when I'm drifting off to sleep. It reminds me of my childhood and the assorted night critters that had sung me to sleep every night. You can hear anything coming, and I have enough warm blankets to get away with it. We don't post guards but let the dogs be our alarms if needed. Even though he usually hangs out with me, tonight, Ajax is off in cabin three with Maya and Kuniko. So, I'm alone with my thoughts, the crickets, and the breeze that's stirring the lake's surface to a shimmering silver playground, visible through the screen door. Bats circle noiselessly, swooping above the surface of the water as they collect their dinner, and I'm entranced by their flight patterns. I pick up a quiet step on the porch's surface, betrayed by a squeak in a board at the top of the stairs no one has ever thought needed fixing, followed by stealthy footfalls. I guess this is one of us, but I reach instinctively for the pistol on the bedside table as a shadow falls between the lake and my bedroom. I'm not sure who it could be, though I have my hopes.

Eve.

Bare legged and wearing a big T-shirt whose color I can't make out, she stands for a moment, silhouetted by the moonlight behind her. She then swings the door open and wordlessly comes over to the bed, and creeps beneath the covers as I scoot sideways to make room. I think way, way back to when we first met, and how we eventually got comfortable after our initial meeting and rough first day, in particular. She came to sleep with me one night back then, just sleep, resting against my body for comfort but facing away. After that, it became periodic—she'd come in at random but always turned in the opposite direction.

This time, she's facing me and slowly slides an arm across my bare chest, her own torso tight to mine, head resting against my shoulder. The moon lights enough of her face for me to see her clearly, and she's smiling.

"Are you okay?" I ask.

"I am now," she whispers.

I am too, at long last.

ABOUT THE AUTHOR

GREG RODE

GREG RODE is the author of the *Sanctuary Chronicles* series. He lives in Cornelius, North Carolina, with his family and two small dogs that aren't nearly as tough as Ajax and Jack.

The cabins and lake described in the novels are real and have been in the family for well over a century. It would indeed be a superb place to go for sanctuary, but there's not enough room for everybody, which is why he doesn't say where it is exactly. That and his grandmother once said not to say where it was if he ever wrote a book there. Since it was very unwise to mess with Grammie, you're on your own when the zombies come.

He is currently working on an epilogue and prequel to the series, though not always at the same time.